C. J. FLOOD

night WANDERERS

SIMON & SCHUSTER

First published in Great Britain in 2016 by Simon & Schuster UK Ltd
A CBS COMPANY

Copyright © 2016 Chelsey Flood

1 3 5 7 9 10 8 6 4 2

Simon & Schuster UK Ltd
1st Floor, 222 Gray's Inn Road
London
WC1X 8HB

www.simonandschuster.co.uk

Simon & Schuster Australia, Sydney
Simon & Schuster India, New Delhi

A CIP catalogue record for this book is available from the British Library.

PB ISBN 978-0-8570-7805-6
eBook ISBN 978-0-8570-7806-3

Typeset in the UK by Hewer Text UK Ltd, Edinburgh
Printed and bound by CPI Group (UK) Ltd, Croydon, CR0 4YY

Simon & Schuster UK Ltd are committed to sourcing paper that is made
from wood grown in sustainable forests and supports the Forest Stewardship
Council, the leading international forest certification organisation. Our
books displaying the FSC logo are printed on FSC certified paper.

For Ursula Freewoman and all my friends.
Live True.

One

Mackerel fishermen found Ti's things on a rock at Durgan Beach early Saturday morning. Black jeans, her beloved long-sleeved dolphin top, grey duffle coat, purse and, round the neck of an empty Bells bottle, the seahorse necklace I bought for her birthday, with its chain broken. Her twin sister's things were there too, though I don't remember what they were exactly.

Ti De Furia was my best friend in the world; Ophelia De Furia was something else completely.

News that the twins were missing tore through Flushing's high street the next day, and the De Furia café shutters stayed down for the first time since they'd opened five years ago. Regulars milled about outside, despondent.

'Beautiful girls, they were.'

'So spirited!'

'No match for Durgan rip tides in a storm.'

Charlie Fielding said she'd seen Ti with a bottle of

whisky the night before when she was running to the Drama block for a forgotten prop. It was show night, so school was busy, and soon others were claiming to have seen Ti stumbling at the edges of the playing field or crying in the car park. Rumours spread fast in Flushing, and after everything that had happened theories developed.

Some kids said the twins had drowned themselves on purpose, to escape all the trouble they'd caused. Others guessed they'd been skinny-dipping drunk and got into danger by mistake. People claimed to have seen the girls hours, minutes, seconds before they disappeared.

It was an accident. A double suicide. A tragedy.

The fact that never changed was that both girls were dead.

I wouldn't believe it, and neither would my little brother Joey. He refused to accept Ti was dead until her body turned up, which made perfect sense to me. We didn't discuss Ophelia – she was unknowable, and capable of anything – but it was nice talking about Ti in the present and future tense.

'She's just hiding out,' Joey told me, lying on my bed waving his feet in the air. He was wearing his dinosaur socks, and I watched the tiny T. rex swaying. 'Waiting for all this to die down, and then – pow!' He slammed his heels down suddenly.

'Pow,' I repeated, and he turned to me so I could see the freckle flecks on his nose.

'She'll emerge like a falcon from the ashes!'

'Phoenix.'

'What?'

'Like a *phoenix* from the ashes.'

'I think they changed it to falcon.'

'They didn't change it to falcon, Joe.'

'They did, Rose, actually. Actually, they did.'

'She's punishing her parents, that's what it is. Her dad's the one that should have drowned.'

'Nobody drowned, Rose. They didn't!'

'I know.'

'And nobody should. Ever!'

'No. I know.'

I put my arm out, and he burrowed into it. They were comforting, these conversations with my brother, even if he was only eight years old, and half convinced he had super powers.

Mum and Dad didn't like it. They whispered to each other about denial and responsibility, and the importance of facing up to the truth, but I no longer listened to what they said.

Joey was the only one who had never given up on Ti, and I loved him for it.

Because if Ti was dead (*which she wasn't*) it was all of our faults.

Two

It all started with a poo in a flower bed. A small act of revenge from Ti, towards our Drama teacher, Ms Chase, for the recent expulsion of Ophelia.

It was dark, with a quarter moon and lots of cloud cover as Ti dashed up the drive of a large semi-detached house, and I followed, adrenalin making the night seem to bounce. It was her turn to wear the purple balaclava we'd found in British Heart Foundation, and I felt strangely conspicuous with my face out in the breeze. A security light clicked on, turning the colours up for a second, and we kept running, past the house and into the depths of the garden. We knew the drill by now: aim for shadows.

Round here, the gardens were huge: five times the size of mine, ten times the size of Ti's. We were on Castle Road where all the rich kids lived, as well as some of the teachers. Lawns and rockeries and netted ponds holding

4

koi carp. Sheds and garages with cars, plural, and conservatories. Lots of trampolines.

The security light clicked off, and we stepped out from a hedge, half blind and clutching each other. Nerves made me need to wee, left laughter right at the top of my throat, and I was already giggling helplessly as Ti led the way across the first garden.

'This way,' she said, tearing over the neat grass. A stepladder helped us over the first fence, an apple tree the second, and the third had only a hedge, which we scrambled through no problem. Black windows loomed over us as we ran, and my guts squirmed because anybody could be looking out – murderers, paedophiles. With my thumping heart, even ghosts seemed possible.

Nightwandering was a hobby of ours, but usually it was aimless. Stealthily dressed we crept from our houses after midnight to explore the town in peace. We lay on the coast path to watch the stars; peed in the long jump sandpit. At night the hierarchies of school ceased to exist, and we were the queens of Flushing.

Nightwandering, my courage almost matched Ti's. But she took risks needlessly.

Using a trampoline to mount a particularly high fence, for instance, when I'd found a perfectly quiet and safe alternative. I winced at the racket she made: creaking springs and stretching canvas, then *crash!* She bellyflopped on top, the whole fence wobbling, her feet scrabbling at the slats of wood as she hauled herself over, shaking with laughter.

I looked around with pathological frequency, pressed into the shadows, expecting lights to come on and our captors to emerge, and then finally Ti landed in the garden with a shaking thud, swearing because she'd bitten her tongue.

'Careful how you go,' she lisped. 'The ground'th wonky.'

A little closer towards the house one of the fence panels was loose, a nail missing from the bottom, and pushing it aside now, I squeezed through, wood scraping the soft skin of my stomach.

'I tried to tell you,' I said, when Ti called me a show-off, and it was true. But Ti had an uncanny ability to turn her ears off when receiving instructions.

'Just hurry up, okay,' I said. 'In, out, remember?'

Ti clutched my wrists, and pressed her forehead to mine. This was our power move, though she used it more often than me.

'This is it,' she whispered, and the wool of her bala-clava was itchy against my skin. Her curly dark hair sprang out of the bottom, instantly recognizable to all who knew her. 'Ms Chase's abode.'

I felt like I was going to collapse. Ms Chase was the kind of teacher who prided herself on not giving second chances. I should have tried harder to talk Ti out of this, but she convinced me that surviving the escapade would make us brave and exciting, and I wanted to be those things so much.

A light came on in a frosted window upstairs, and my blood pumped so hard it made me dizzy.

'Careful,' I pleaded, as Ti crept towards the house, unshaken by the proof that Chase was inside. There was no way I was going any closer if I could help it. Upstairs, the light went out, and my stomach fizzed with nerves as Ti looked around for the perfect place to take her revenge. Stepping into a flower bed, she whipped down her black jeans, and I was confronted with a full view of her bum.

'Don't look,' she said at the same time as I said, 'Jesus!'

'You say "don't look" *before* you pull your pants down, Ti. Like a second or two *before*, not after.'

Ti farted in response. I couldn't believe it when she did things like this; it was like she didn't care what anyone thought of her, and that impressed me more than anything. She and Ophelia were exactly the same in this respect, though they showed it in different ways. They'd inherited it from their dad, Fabio, who shouted instead of talking, and swore like an angry chef (which he was).

'I don't know if I can go,' Ti whispered. 'I don't know if I've got anything.'

'You can do it, Ti. I believe in you.'

'I'm not sure,' she said, 'the cupboards might be bare,' and her voice as she strained was gross, but it only made us laugh harder. I'd told her to bring toilet roll, but she'd insisted she didn't need it on account of her gift for doing what she referred to as 'ghost poos'.

My shoulders shook, and the urge to pee was strong, but I daren't go here, in spite of Ti's encouragement. 'It's the most natural thing in the world!' she said. 'Don't be such a prude.' All the same, I couldn't do it. Not in a teacher's garden.

We were having fun again now, but still I counted down the seconds until we could leave. I pictured us safely on the coast path, sharing out the tea in Ti's rucksack.

'*What are you doing? Stop!*' I hissed, because she'd promised to leave as soon as she'd delivered her present. Downstairs the lamps were dim, floral blinds down. The faintest glow escaped, lighting up Ti who had crept forwards and now was metres from the window, trying to look in.

'Sexy music!' Ti hissed back. 'She's got someone in there!'

Her voice shook with delight, and I knew from experience there was no getting through to her now. For the first time in the history of nightwandering I wished to be tucked up in bed, with a nice sensible friend who liked to sleep at night after watching a film with a face mask or

8

maybe plaiting each other's hair, and then Ti took another step.

The tin clatter was deafening against the moon-quiet night. The metal dog bowl she'd stood in spinning round and round.

Click! The garden flooded with electric light.

All in the same second Ti stopped laughing, I sprang for the loose fence panel, and Chase appeared at the patio doors in a lilac satin dressing gown.

Ti backed away, but it was too late. Chase had stepped on to the decking outside her house. She clutched her gown at the neck, red feathered hair loose around her narrow shoulders, and it was so private seeing her like that I almost closed my eyes.

'Titania?' Chase said, disbelieving. She insisted on using Ti's full name, and pronouncing it in this fancy way – Tih-tahn-yuh – completely different to Fab's version – Tie-tan-yuh – and it drove Ti doolally, though perhaps she wasn't thinking too hard about that right then.

I was outside the pool of light, the palm trees beside the house providing cover, but I could hardly breathe. Any second Chase could walk from her spotlit patio and catch me.

She couldn't finish sentences. 'What . . . ? How . . . ? I don't . . .'

I inched forward, the grass crunching ear-splittingly with every step.

9

'*What* in god's name are you doing in my garden?' Chase said, getting herself together at last. 'This isn't funny, Titania. Don't think this can be shrugged off as a prank. I've called the police!'

At the mention of police I pushed the loose plank aside, and squeezed back through the gap into the garden with the trampoline. Before I'd even thought about my decision, I'd sprinted into the road and was crouching behind a car, panting.

With my fingers crossed, I waited for Ti to emerge with the defiant look she wore at school, the closest she got to a uniform, but she never came out. Finally, a police car arrived, and if I'd dared to look up as it left, I would have seen Ti, ashen, in the back seat.

Three

Whenever I heard the word *kindred*, I thought of me and Ti. It was a rainy Monday in Year Six when she turned up in my classroom. She was big-boned and fear-less-looking, with short dark curly hair that stood out all around her face. She'd moved from Italy, Mrs Gamble said, and so at break the kids made fun of her accent, and tasselled leather shoes, and the extra vowels she put after words when she talked.

She didn't run shrieking to the veranda like the rest of us girls when it started raining, but stood face to the sky, and let herself get drenched. After dinner, when Mrs Gamble paired us together, I was secretly pleased. I could be trusted to be helpful and kind, Mrs Gamble said, but the intense look she gave made me wonder if she knew how I longed for someone who thought I was brilliant all the time. Unlike Charlie Fielding who laughed with Mia Lewis whenever I got upset.

My nerves sparked with excitement as Titania and Charlie swapped seats. Ti was still damp from her soaking, dark hair tamed into ringlets, and her toffee-coloured eyes were open and amused. She wrote questions on a piece of paper that we passed back and forth, demanding to know why everyone stared at her, and wore the same shoes, and followed Charlie Fielding with a frightened expression.

Do you follow CF? she wrote, and my answer covered the whole reverse side of A4: *NO.*

Charlie cursed our alliance. She banned us from sitting at the good table at dinner, and made sure we were picked last for teams in PE. She invented lies about why Ti had moved here, and called me a traitor for leaving her gang, but I didn't mind.

I'd never had a true friend before, and I knew it. Charlie had always made me feel less than I was, whereas Ti made me feel like more. She didn't say it was disgusting if I had gravy on my school tie or sleep in my eye, and she didn't want to talk all day about the clothes everyone was wearing. Best of all she loved school dinners just as much as me.

Ti and me were outcasts, and I'd never been happier.

She was used to it, she said, because her dad got people's backs up wherever he went.

'We're a family of outcasts,' she said. 'You'll see.'

And I did. Within weeks Fab had annoyed the Flushingites by feeding leftover ciabattas from the café

12

to the seagulls in the square. The first time he didn't know it was an offence, but after he was prosecuted it became a regular act of pure De Furia rebellion.

'Look at them!' he said fondly, when a small colony hopped towards us on the pier. 'The way they jerk their necks, just like little Mafiosi – who could resist you, eh? Little brutes! Landed in the wrong place!'

Checking the coast was clear in an exaggerated fashion, he scattered a handful of chips, while Ti's shy mum, June, first waved her arms at the birds, then collected the chips he'd thrown and put them in the bin.

Everyone felt sorry for June. Fab strode around the town like he'd always been there, with his bright checked trousers and loud remarks, and June scurried behind him, sending out apologetic looks and wincing. They were an odd match, people said.

Which were my sentiments exactly about Ti and her sister. I didn't even know she was an identical twin until Ophelia turned up in Mr Burgoine's class a week later.

'Nobody notices me when Ophelia's around,' Ti confessed when I called her out on how weird it was, and though I'd never admit it she wasn't exaggerating. Ti was pretty if you stopped to look, but Ophelia's beauty *made* you stop and look. Both girls had wide cheeks and full mouths and thick eyebrows over melty brown eyes, but every time Ophelia's features arranged

13

themselves in the slightly more attractive way: her eyes slanted upwards where Ti's were more square, her front teeth had a gap where Ti's were close together, plus she was skinny (because she rarely ate), and like me Ti still had what Mum insisted was only puppy fat.

Seeing she was destined to be popular, Charlie immediately tried to take Ophelia under her wing, but Ophelia was too powerful. She burst straight through the feathers, and the two of them began their drama-filled friendship. I hated it when they fell out because Ophelia came to hang around with us; she spoke Italian to exclude me, and Ti stopped laughing at my silliest jokes, pretending to be mature and nonchalant like her sister.

They both despised being referred to as *the twins* or being asked if they felt each other's pain, but they had a strange power over each other, and almost psychic ways of communicating, and I was painfully jealous of their bond.

Still, I never would have thought it would make us lose touch.

Four

Ti was in the middle of explaining what had happened in Chase's garden to a disbelieving gaggle of classmates, when a smug-looking prefect called Ethan Crisp came for her. It was the end of Registration and Charlie Fielding and her horrible boyfriend Alex Riviere were thrilled, grinning and wiggling their eyebrows as she packed up her stuff.

After abandoning Ti on Saturday night, all I wanted was a chance to explain, but she hadn't let me. She'd talked on and on, and I couldn't get a word in, so I knew her feelings were hurt. I hadn't even been able to tell her I'd called her house first thing Sunday morning, before they all started work at the café, she was gabbing so much.

Fab had hung up on me without saying anything, and when I called back Ophelia had said one word before doing the same.

Coward.

I hated to think what poison she'd have been spitting in Ti's ears about me since then.

Alisha Patel and Kiaru Aki gave me sympathetic looks as I blinked back tears, puzzling it over. Alisha was chubby, with a film-star-pretty face, and Kiaru was the only boy in our year with long hair that wasn't to do with surfing; the only Japanese kid too. I'd started out in the same sets as them, but I couldn't keep up, and though they rarely talked to me (too wrapped up in each other) I got the impression they were sympathetic.

Walking alone down the drive after school, I begged the universe for Ti to be all right. To have been sent home for the day or, at worst, suspended, and for her dad to have gone easy on her. I walked slowly so I wouldn't have to overtake Charlie and Alex and the Drama lot up ahead, but when they stopped to practise the cheesiest dance routine of all time I had no choice. Joey would be coming out of Fairfields Juniors any minute, and since that horrible Monday when Mum couldn't make it, he got scared if nobody was there to pick him up.

'Oh, wifey!' Alex called as soon as he noticed me, his Nike rucksack slung over one of his broad shoulders. 'Where's your little wifey?'

Flamethrowers lit up my cheeks, and I pretended to search in my bag for something to keep my face hidden, praying they wouldn't notice my blush; that it wasn't as dramatic-looking as it felt. Alex had been obsessed with Ophelia for years, before he got together with Charlie, and now he made a point of being awful to me and Ti, as though to prove his loyalty.

Charlie laughed too loud when he did it, and the whole thing made me queasy. She flicked her blonde hair now, and covered her face to hide how hard she was faking.

The main reason we had been friends in the first place was because our mums knew each other from university. They had played hockey together every Tuesday until September last year when Mum had cancelled because of what we thought then was flu. Sophie Fielding was the only one from the team who still called occasionally to ask if Mum was well enough for a game, and I loved her for it. Last week, Charlie had written a message in the get-well-soon card her mum sent, and my mum had almost cried she was so touched.

'Aw, she's blushing. It must be love!' Charlie said now, and I gave her a baffled look because her behaviour made absolutely no sense to me.

'She's Rosie Bloooooooom,' Alex said, and Mia Lewis and all the other Drama dimwits fell about laughing.

The joke never got old because my cheeks never stopped providing the punchline. I'd googled how to change my name by deed poll, but couldn't follow through because my parents thought it was *perfect*. They talked about nominative determinism and Dickens, and other academic stuff that went over my head, and I just didn't have the stomach to break it to them, that since puberty they'd basically been in cahoots with my biggest detractors.

I caught Charlie's eye as I passed, hoping her grin might slip, and it did. Mum was always trying to convince me that she was insecure, and I should feel sorry for her, and it was difficult because she was so pretty and rich, but in that second, for the first time, I almost managed it.

Five

Joey belted out of the classroom with the hood of his blue coat draped over his head and my mood lifted completely. He knocked other kids out of the way, making machine-gun noises, and I felt the tangle of humiliation and anxiety in my stomach unravelling.

Girls and boys smiled as he passed, calling out to him as though they liked using his name. A skinny ginger girl called Lara couldn't take her eyes off him. She called bye repeatedly in a soft, eager little voice that he didn't seem to notice.

'Rosie!' he shouted, launching himself at my belly for a hug.

His head bobbed at my waist as he grinned up at me, purple ink on one cheek, beginning a monologue about the games he'd played at break time and how Lara wrote in his spelling book by mistake, which was really annoying because he was hoping to finish Year Four without any writing in it at all.

'You know what, Joe?' I told him sincerely. 'You're already cooler than me.'

At home I made him a cucumber sandwich, and took Mum's tea and toast up in record speed so that I could ring Ti. Fab answered again, and I begged him not to hang up.

'She doesn't talk on the phone any more,' he said in his booming Italian-tinged way. Ti and Ophelia had lost their accents, but for Fab almost every word still ended with a vowel. 'Or go out. Or have friends. So you'd better just forget her.'

He hung up, and my stomach turned with nerves. Fab got angry fast, but it passed quickly too, like a jet: big noise then nothing. Was it that bad what had happened? I couldn't cope with Ti being mad at me for long.

Watching telly in the living room, I couldn't follow the show. Sometimes Ti could sneak a call, if her parents were busy with washing tablecloths or preparing dishes for the café the next day. If not she had to wait until they had gone to bed, and then Dad got mad about her ringing late and waking Mum, which was completely unfair because what else could she do? A queasy feeling told me she didn't want to call at all.

Dad got home around ten, out of breath and gasping for a drink of water. He had biro notes scribbled all over his hands, and a smudge of ink on his nose, and he hugged me when I opened the oven and took out a jacket potato for him. His hair was completely grey, but he still wore it long and in a side parting, like his and Mum's music heroes.

'I've been on the phone all day,' he said, chugging from the tap before going into one of his speeches about the indignity of begging for money at his age. I wasn't entirely sure what his current campaign was, something about greedy landlords and second homes, but I hoped he might notice something was the matter with me and ask if I wanted to talk, like he did when Joey was quiet, but he just set about buttering his potato, unloading the dryer between mouthfuls, and then making up Mum's night-time tray, and I couldn't bring myself to interrupt.

It had been six months now without a diagnosis. An invisible disease that meant headaches and sleep that didn't refresh and, for me and Joe, endlessly being told to *shhhhh*. Mum used to teach Psychology at the university and make salsa verde and tuna steak, and go for runs around the castle. Now she rarely got out of bed. Dad and me shared the chores we couldn't avoid between us, while Joey simply made more for us to do.

Mum had loads of visitors at first, but people stopped coming round when it didn't seem like she was getting better. She said she didn't mind, that she was worn out with everybody joking how they could do with a few weeks in bed, or saying how their colleague claimed to have the same thing, except they were just lazy.

'I bet they say the same about me,' she would say after they'd gone. 'Stupid invisible illness!'

She would roll over then, exhausted by the interaction and fall into a deep and sudden sleep, as if to prove she for one wasn't faking. Her eyes looked bruised with shadow, and I couldn't imagine her laughing, and I *missed* her. Dad was great, but he didn't know what being a teenage girl was like. When I finally got my period over Christmas, he sent me in to the Co-op to buy my first box of tampons for myself, even though Charlie's handsome older brother Will was working the till, and would know for certain I had a *vagina*.

'There's absolutely nothing to be embarrassed about,' Dad had said, his ears bright red, as I jumped in the car with the offending article and ordered him to drive, for god's sake, drive. Mum didn't get embarrassed about anything. The flamethrowers were definitely a gift from Dad.

Mum's illness was the main reason that on Sunday morning, after nightmares about crashing in a police car Ti was driving, I'd woken in a blind panic. The illness fed on effort and stress. It was sinister and unpredictable, and it liked to punish Mum when she tried to defeat it. Like on my birthday, when she'd seemed better, and asked if I wanted to go into town to choose a gift.

It was like old times – walking down the high street together, breathing out mist as we talked about what to get Dad and Joey for Christmas. Her hair was the colour of horse chestnuts, same as mine, and it looked so pretty against her cream woolly hat that I decided to grow my hair super long too. It had just passed my shoulders for the first time since I was a little kid.

We drank mochas at The Jam because the music's always good there, and everything was fine until Mum fainted at WHSmith while I was choosing a new album. Dad had to come home from university to pick us up, and when she was safely back in bed he told me I should have known better.

'We can't be selfish, Rosie; we've got to be a team. I need you on my side, because at the moment, I'm afraid your mum doesn't know what's best for her.'

The whole fortnight after, she didn't make it out of bed once. What if *I'd* been brought home by the police? I had to be more careful. No more silly risk-taking. I picked flowers from the garden, then dug out my art box so Joey could make a get-well card. She mustn't think we'd given up on her too.

At half past ten Dad insisted I go up to bed as usual, because it was a school night, he said, but really it was so

23

he could use the internet uninterrupted. He was addicted to ranting in forums, though he claimed it was an important part of his activism.

'Can I stay up a bit longer?' I said. 'Ti's going to call.'

'What can you possibly have left to say to each other? You've been together all day.'

This was his usual grumble, and I wanted to tell him he was wrong, that we hadn't been together all day – that was the problem – but I wasn't keen to let on that Ti was in trouble again if I didn't have to. Mum and Dad already had their doubts about our friendship.

'*Bed*,' he snapped, running out of patience without warning, like he did sometimes lately, but there was no way I would get to sleep if I didn't know how Ti was, so I lay on the landing instead, looking up at the paper moon lightshade, willing the phone to ring.

'Swings, midnight,' Ti's voice whispered when it finally did, and I was so relieved to hear her and know she wasn't mad with me that I forgot all about my promise to be more careful, and after setting my alarm for fifty-five minutes' time, I fell into a deep and peaceful sleep.

Six

The Beacon was at the top of a hill precisely between my terrace and Ti's estate, and we often met there at midnight. Ti's parents were unconscious then, which meant she had more freedom. Her family were even more demanding than mine, and when she wasn't at school they had her polishing cutlery or straining tomato sauce or laminating new menus for the café.

Ti was there already, sitting on top of the slide, in her black jeans and dolphin top, looking out at the view. She'd taken her make-up off, and let her hair down from the teddy-bear buns it had been in when I'd seen her briefly at school, and she looked younger without the usual trimmings.

Seeing me, she bowed her head, and my stomach churned. I scrambled up the red climbing net to where she sat, cross-legged, picking at what was left of her nail varnish.

'Hey,' she said, but she didn't smile or hug me as usual, and she seemed to be in her own world more than mine. She shoved a chunk of her thick curly hair behind an ear, and stared at the little black spots of varnish on her fingernails, and I waited.

From the top of the slide at the Beacon, you had the best view in town. You could see where the river met the sea, and the boats swayed in the harbour, as well as the cranes in the docks just round the headland. I had more pictures of this view at sunset than I knew what to do with, but I couldn't stop taking them.

Mum had made me sign four before she had them framed and hung them on the stairs to their bedroom in the attic. Walking up there I felt proud, like I was already a famous photographer.

'What happened?' I managed eventually, and Ti shook her head, and took a breath.

'I'm out. Chase told Kes that I threatened her.'

'No!'

'The police gave me a warning, and Dad's not talking to me.'

'Oh, Ti.'

'I feel so stupid. I was so mad about them getting rid of Ophelia, and now I've gone and got myself chucked out too.'

Ti breathed out her nose in a disheartened way, and I held her hand, and picked at the black speck of nail varnish at the centre of her thumbnail because I didn't know what to say.

'So what happened? *Exactly.*'

'Chase was in Kes's office when I got there, sitting on a seat behind his desk with him – in case I didn't already know it was two against one – and he started talking about how seriously Fairfields takes the safety of its teachers and students, and how there's zero tolerance to violence or the threat of violence at this school . . .'

'And what was Chase doing?'

'I don't know. I daren't look at her. It was so embarrassing. I thought they might have found the poo, and that I was going to have to explain it. I didn't dare look at anyone, I just stared at my lap the whole time.

'And then Kes brought up the police, and the seriousness of trespassing on people's private property, and I felt like a really creepy stalker, but I couldn't think of anything to say that wouldn't make things worse. I couldn't think of anything that would explain it, because how could I explain about nightwandering?'

I squeezed her hand, wanting to make her feel better, and like I definitely wasn't thinking *I told you so* because I'd warned her not to go near the house, and she hadn't listened to me, and now here we were.

'The way Kes told it, I was in Chase's garden to intimidate her. That's why I went there. But we were just messing around! I was laughing the whole time, wasn't I?'

'And she said you threatened her? What did she say you said?'

Ti nodded sadly, watching my hands as I turned hers over, looking for more varnish to pick. 'I can't remember. It was like having an out-of-body experience. Like, all this time I've been determined to make it through to the end of school, but underneath I'd known really that I wouldn't, that there'd be *something*, and it was so weird. I felt like I was watching myself on telly.'

I was just holding her hand now, and our palms were sweating, but I didn't want to let go.

'It's because of Ophelia. They think I'm the same as her. I wish she wasn't my sister sometimes, I really do. She ruins everything.'

I kept my mouth firmly shut.

Ophelia had been expelled a week ago after a culmination of things, but the first big one was an incident last month at the *Grease* rehearsals when Charlie ended up with a split lip. Ophelia said it was an accident, that she'd lost her footing in the dance they were learning, and that she hadn't meant to knock anyone off the stage, but Charlie was having none of it, and, in the end, the tension got so bad that Chase told Ophelia she didn't have the right attitude required to put on a production.

'Honestly, Rosie, it was so odd. I didn't realize what

was going on. I mean, I still thought I was just being told off. I was waiting for the punishment, but Kes was talking about my general attitude, and lateness. My marks. That I've not written a single word in my Geography workbook.

'He had to really spell it out to me. "So, I'm going to have to ask you to leave, Titania." And I was like, *Okay, phew!* And I jumped out my seat, thinking of coming to find you in English, and he must have known I didn't understand, because he said it again really slowly: "I'm going to have to ask you to leave school property. We think The Bridge might be a better fit."

'And it was really sad because I'd always thought he liked me. He gave me bourbons if I got sent to him, and let me chat about stuff instead of doing whatever boring work I'd been given . . .'

The Bridge was where they sent kids that couldn't get on with the rules and regulations of normal school. The idea was that once you'd improved a bit you could return to a conventional school, if you could find one that would take you, but all the kids there were such troublemakers that hardly anyone got the chance. Ophelia had lasted three days before she'd begged her mum and dad to let her be 'home-schooled', i.e. work full time in the café.

'Kes actually came with me, you know. He escorted me off the property, like I was dangerous.'

My anxiety was building as it dawned on me that there was something I could do to help, something real, which Ti would do in a blink if this situation was reversed. I could confess that I had been there too.

'Can they actually do that though?' I said, stalling. 'Can they just chuck you off whenever they feel like it? I mean, don't they have to speak to your parents?'

'He already had. Mum knew all about it when I got home. She'd refused to come and get me because Monday's Pensioners' Special.'

Ti looked so worried fiddling with her silver seahorse necklace. She put it in her mouth then dropped it, then put it in her mouth again. Staring out at the horizon, she didn't seem to see anything, and I squeezed her hand, but it was limp in mine.

'Ti?' I said, moving my face to be near hers, wanting her to come back. 'Hey.'

Her brown laughing eyes were so blank that I froze.

'*Hey,*' I said, again, rubbing her arm.

'I'm no good, Rosie,' she said, head sinking.

'Don't say that, Ti. Of course you are. Hey, Ti, don't say that!' But she wouldn't lift her head no matter what I did.

'I'm broken.'

'You aren't broken, Ti, Chase lied. Listen to me, you aren't broken!'

'I hate myself,' she said, and I had to strain to hear her.

'Why do you even want to be friends with me?' she said, finally, in a quiet voice I wasn't used to, and I felt my eyes widen with the shock of it. 'I know I bring this stuff on myself. I could hear you calling me back, but I just went on anyway. And then . . . It's like I want bad stuff to happen, Rosie. I mean, what's wrong with me? Is it in my blood?'

Her voice was so small, I couldn't bear it. 'It's not in your blood, Ti, you just made a mistake. We can fix it. Listen to me, we can fix it.'

I thought back to Saturday afternoon when she'd made us go down this slide together though we were much too big. Little kids had laughed while parents tutted, and I wished we could rewind to that moment. I wanted to slide down the metal chute clutching her waist, my hair lifting from the back of my neck, and later, when we walked home to her house for tea, I wanted to tell her *no*, I wouldn't go to Chase's garden, because it was a stupid idea, and I needed to be sensible for the sake of my mum, that she couldn't afford to get into any more trouble.

But I hadn't done that. I'd gone with her, and laughed along at her tricks, and it wasn't fair I should get away with it.

'I'll tell Kes I was with you,' I said before I could change my mind.

Ti lifted her head. 'No, Rosie . . .'

31

'I'll say we were messing about, that we didn't even know it was her house . . .'

'But I was the one that—'

'You shouldn't have to take all the blame,' I said, because it was the truth, and I wanted to be strong like she was. Wind blew the still leafless branches of the trees at the edge of the park, and the cloud overhead was suffocating, but as Ti wrapped her arms round me, and I breathed in the pina colada smell of her shampoo, I swore I would do anything to make her feel better.

Seven

By Registration news had spread about Ti's expulsion, and Charlie Fielding was enjoying herself.

'Why don't you leave with her?' she said, sliding into Ti's empty seat beside me. 'Nobody would miss you, you know.'

The rest of our form listened intrigued as Charlie told how Ti had threatened Chase with a knife, and how Ms Chase was getting an injunction against her.

'That isn't what happened,' I said, but my cheeks were on fire, and nobody wanted to hear my version of events when Charlie's was so much more thrilling. I couldn't make my voice heard over the excitable gaggle, and embarrassed I gave up.

'I know the *whole* story,' Charlie explained. 'Because Ms Chase told Will.'

Charlie's brother Will was a sixth-former now, and no longer allowed to star in the school play, so Chase

33

had made him director. Will took the role dispropor-
tionately seriously, carrying a *Grease*-themed clipboard,
and smoothing his golden hair into a fifties T-Bird quiff
every day.

He had the same very defined cupid's bow mouth as
Charlie, and most of the girls at school had at least a
vague crush on him.

'So how was it being married to a stalker?' Alex asked,
turning to me in a way that made it clear he expected an
answer. Charlie had left Ti's seat now, and was at the
front of the class, leaning on Alex, eyes gleaming as she
waited for my response.

'You should know,' I said, because Charlie had been
chasing Alex since Year Seven, and hadn't got a look in
until Ophelia was out of the way. Charlie looked down,
muttering obscenities, and Alex put his arm round her.
I could feel my concealer bubbling like lava, but it felt
good to hit back. Especially when I saw Kiaru and Alisha
covering their mouths as they laughed.

Ophelia was still a sore point. Last week there had
been a row because Will had taken to wearing Alex's
leather jacket from the costume department around
school. Alex had had a go at him about it, and then
Charlie got upset because she thought the argument was
really about Ophelia. She accused Alex of resenting her
brother for stealing Ophelia from him, even though
Ophelia and Alex had never been anything more than

friends. That was the strange thing about the Drama lot, you heard all their news, whether you cared or not.

'Blooooooom,' Alex breathed, in the specific way he had developed, and Charlie laughed, clutching his arm, but I could see her desperation. I went over and over what I would say to Kes, how I'd clear Ti's name, and stop the rumours, and it was a relief for us all when Mr Miles arrived to call the register.

Eight

'Enter,' Kes called almost immediately after I knocked at lunchtime break. We called him Kes because he hovered over everything like a bird of prey. And because he had a huge nose. Tall and imposing, he liked to walk into lessons without warning.

He sat, writing in a notebook, behind a huge desk covered in curiosities, tribal-looking wood carvings of naked people and a sheep's skull as well as a small glass dome encasing what looked like a stuffed mole. Ti thought it might be his power animal.

'What can I do for you ...?' He paused, confirming my suspicion that he didn't know who I was.

'Rosie. Rosie Bloom.'

I had put on extra concealer because I sensed a day of heavy blushing, and though my voice was coming out at a duckling's volume, at least I was here. My toes ached from clenching them so hard, but I hadn't run. Yet.

'Ah, yes, *Rosie*.' He smiled, as if all of the heart-warming moments we had shared were coming back to him, and it was hard to tell whether he really knew who I was or not.

I searched for my opener, but it was gone, evaporated in the impatience of Kes's stare.

'So . . . ?'

'Um, you just expelled my best friend,' I blurted out.

'Ah, I see.' Kes returned the lid to his pen, and sat back in his chair.

'And I think it might have been unfair,' I said, and the way he blinked at me, as though surprised, reminded me of my dad – slightly uncomfortable but eager to please – and it made me feel more confident.

'It just seems like it's one person's word against another, and that maybe—'

'Hold on!' he said, and he was no longer my dad, he was the headmaster of my school, the person with the power to make me join Ti at The Bridge. He held his index finger out like a warning. 'Hold it *right there*, Rosie Bloom. Your friend, Titania—' (He pronounced it like Chase: Tih-tahn-yuh.)

'Ti—'

'Yes, *Titania*, has not contributed to the fabric of the school environment for the last three years. She's been in and out of my office like it was a tuck shop. Good girl, but not academic. Not Fairfields material. I've spoken to her teachers, and they are in agreement. The

37

Bridge will be a better fit; they're less strict there, less demanding. She doesn't contribute in lessons, she talks constantly, uninvited, and when she does answer a question it's rarely an appropriate response.'

'But she didn't get chance to explain, not properly, and Ms Chase—'

The finger came up again to shush me, and I resented it, but I stopped talking too, because I could hear my voice, and it was shaking and high, and who was going to take me seriously?

'Miss Bloom,' he said, 'are you here looking for trouble?'

He blinked again, and his grey eyes were severe as I took a breath, preparing myself. In five seconds I would confess.

Five.

'Because your friend Titania, I'm afraid, was. We pride ourselves on allowing our students freedom, but some are not responsive to this. Your friend didn't take her education seriously. In fact, I have it on good authority that she did not contribute anything very positive to the Fairfields community at all. Ms Chase on the other hand—'

Four.

I rolled my eyes. Here it came.

'*Ms Chase* has breathed life into our Drama department. She has grown a broken piano, some rusty triangles and the odd maraca into something close to an orchestra. And how do you think these instruments and materials turn up? It's all a matter of Ms Chase's tireless campaigning, her resourcefulness and fundraising, her connections.'

Three.

'She made eight hundred and thirteen pounds for the Drama department last term. Eight hundred and thirteen pounds! Now *that's* the way to perform at school. *That's* the way to contribute.'

Two.

His eyes had sort of glazed over, and I wondered if he'd forgotten who he was talking to, and why he was making this speech. The finger rose again, and I watched it dance, wanting something to pin my eyes to.

One.

'I was in the garden with her.'

That's what I should have said, and maybe I would have if Kes hadn't said what he did next.

'Your parents expect more from you, Rosie, and I know for a fact that there's enough on the family plate at the moment without extra trouble. With a good support system behind you, you could do very well here, if you'd only stop resting on your laurels and apply yourself.'

Kes's grey eyes burned into mine, and I swallowed. He really did know who I was!

'You're a good student, Rosie; we should be expecting As from you. See this as a chance to start over, make new friends. Take a leaf from Ms Chase's book: set your sights on *exceptional.*'

Nine

I still hadn't found a way to tell my parents about Ti's expulsion when Dad ordered me up to Mum's room on Wednesday evening.

'*Now*, Rosie,' he insisted, and my guts tingled.

They knew.

Now I would have to answer thousands of impossible questions like: why did Ti think it was okay to creep around at night, and why did I think it was okay to keep secrets from them, and why wouldn't I make friends with the well-behaved, hardworking kids who got top marks and kept their parents in the loop? All of which would segue effortlessly into the main problem they had with Ti – the main problem they had with me – which was that we didn't take schoolwork seriously.

Mum was propped up in bed, and it was stuffy in there in spite of the lavender oil she constantly burned. Her long hair was freshly washed and clipped on top of her head, and her skin looked pale and fresh, making me wish for the millionth time I'd inherited her complexion instead of dad's.

She patted the space beside her, and reluctantly I sat down. Dad took the armchair in the corner, and I looked from one to the other of them, trying to work out who was less angry.

Mum's expression was caring, and I resisted the urge to tell all. First lesson of adolescence: wait and see what they know. Ti taught me that.

'We heard about Titania,' Mum said. 'Dad bumped into Soph at the shops.'

'She called your mum afterwards,' he said quickly in response to my glare.

'Why didn't you tell us, Rose?' Mum said, and she seemed more hurt than angry, unlike Dad. I focused my attention on her. These days, she was the softer touch.

'I didn't want you to worry,' I said, and Mum spluttered, then shot an accusing look at Dad.

'I'm not *entirely* useless, you know. You can still come to me.'

I looked at my hands then, because I didn't want her to see in my face how completely untrue that was.

In the hallway I could hear a very light rustling – Joey listening, no doubt. He was a little ninja. I'd taught him everything he knew.

'I mean it, Rosie – maybe I am physically useless, but you can still talk to me. I'm still your mum, aren't I? What's up?'

I looked at Dad.

'Don't check with him! *I'm* telling you, you can talk to me. I *want* you to talk to me. *Please*. I'm begging.'

'It's just that you always think so badly of Ti. I didn't want to give you anything extra.'

'We don't think badly of Ti,' Mum said, and I rubbed my face with exasperation. Why couldn't she just be honest?

'Well, you don't think she's a good influence, do you? *I do worse in the lessons we're together . . . I might work harder if I had more academic friends . . .* Don't deny it now; you've said it hundreds of times.'

'Maybe we have a point . . .' she conceded.

Dad looked at the carpet. He was impressed by Ti's non-conformity, and in the past he'd joined me in sticking up for her, but it was clear he wouldn't today. They had already prepped for the encounter, and I felt left out. Everyone had somebody except for me now.

Rustling again in the corridor, and I hoped Joey *was* listening, that way I could complain to him afterwards without having to join the dots. He thought Ti was the best thing since dinosaur eggs. She was the only person beside him that genuinely thought jellyfish were interesting. The two of them had tank-stared for hours when we had Joey's birthday at the aquarium.

42

Under pressure from Mum's eyes, Dad put on his parenting voice, which was annoying given that I was more of a parent in the household than either of them lately, but I kept hold of my temper because I didn't want to make anyone feel worse.

'If we *do* think badly of Ti, it's only because of the number of stories we hear about her getting into trouble. You're in Year Ten now; you'll be sitting your GCSEs next year – it's time to focus.'

Mum nodded, but her attention was flagging, and Dad glowered at me like let's hurry this along.

'You really don't need to worry,' I said. 'I'm going to get my head down and work. I don't have any friends to distract me now anyway . . .' I meant this last bit as a joke, but saying it I felt sorry for myself, and it came out petulant.

'That's unfair, Rosie!' Mum said. 'You *know* we want you to have friends. All we said about Ti was that perhaps you were too close, that perhaps you could have other friends as well. And she isn't the *most* hardworking girl in the world, you've got to admit . . . Sophie said Charlie—'

'Never listen to anything Sophie Fielding says, Mum! Charlie's so jealous of Ophelia she can't even be friends with anyone who talks to her any more.'

Mum tilted her head. 'I know Sophie's not exactly the most neutral source at the BBC, but—'

'See, you've listened to her! You can't listen to her. Anyone but her, Mum, seriously.'

'Rosie, if you don't tell us what happens, we have no choice but to get our news from other people.'

'Just not Sophie Fielding!'

'She's only looking out for her daughter, Rosie. Charlie's had a difficult year . . .'

'Honestly, Mum, Charlie Fielding does not need protecting. She's a bully. All that stuff that happened with Ophelia was Charlie winding her up. She was asking for it!'

'No one is ever "asking" to be physically attacked, Rosie,' Mum said. 'The De Furias might think shouting and violence is acceptable, but the Blooms don't. We think it's important not to upset each other in this household. "Asking for it." You mustn't say that. It makes you sound ignorant. We've brought you up better.'

I was so frustrated I leapt from the bed. Forget how tired she was, I was tired too. She was sympathetic to everyone but Ti.

'Charlie Fielding is a snake, Mum.'

'*Rosie*—'

'She is. If you knew her properly, if you *saw* her at school . . .'

'I know you've had your fallings out, but whenever I see her she says how she wishes you could put the past behind you. She's made mistakes like anyone else. She's not such a bad kid. She always makes me a cup of tea when I visit – used to visit – and tells me about rehearsals, all that, and she's *so* good to her mum. You should give her a chance. Especially now Ti's left.'

'She's an actress, Mum. You shouldn't believe a word that comes out her mouth. Charlie Fielding is a bitch, pure and true.'

'Rosie! You can't call people that! Especially girls. Remember the *sisterhood*.'

'Mum, there is no sisterhood. I'm really sorry. It's a nice idea, but it doesn't exist. Not at secondary school.'

'But you used to be so close!'

'We were only "close" while I went along with everything she said. She's a nasty snake, and you shouldn't trust her. I'm actually being very restrained here, Mum. The B-word is a very PG way of expressing how I feel about Charlie Fielding.'

Mum closed her eyes, and I knew I'd said too much, but how was I supposed to remember? The whole thing about Mum had always been that she was genuinely up for discussion. She *loved* changing her mind; it made her feel enlightened. She didn't care about being right at all costs like most people. Like Dad.

'You're right,' she would say mid-argument, the moment it dawned on her. 'I get it now. I thought I was right, but it's you. Clever girl!'

She'd even thank me for showing her the way, and

then we'd *both* feel enlightened. It wasn't like that now, though. Her voice had weakened the way it did these days, and I felt bad for pushing her.

'I know you love Ti, and she's been good to you, helping you stick up for yourself, and looking out for you, but you have to understand that we can't ignore behaviour like this. The girl has problems, Rosie. Even you've admitted as much.'

'I said she doesn't always have the easiest home life, her family put her under pressure from time to time . . .'

Mum looked at Dad in a way that made me nervous, and he took over again.

'We don't think it's a good idea for you to spend time with her any more, not for a while at least. Until she's pulled herself together a little bit.'

'No!'

'Just while the dust settles . . .'

'You're so obsessed with the fact that she's a bad influence that you don't see how she's a good influence, how much she helps me! And what if I'm a good influence on her? What if stopping me from seeing her makes everything worse?'

'It's not your responsibility to keep Titania's behaviour in check,' Mum said. 'Her parents should be doing that.'

'Well, what if *I'm* the bad influence?'

Mum laughed then. 'Bloody sneaky bad influence if it's you.'

Dad joined in. He tried not to, but he couldn't help it, and I wanted to tell them that they were wrong about me, that I wasn't the good girl they thought. That I walked the town at night with Ti. I'd been in Chase's garden. *I* lied to *them* too. But what would it achieve? To say I was a liar and a wimp, not the person they thought at all, when their eyes glowed with love and here Mum was actually laughing.

'I'm sorry,' Mum said. 'We aren't laughing at you, we want what's best for you, we just . . .'

She winced slightly and rubbed at her temples, another headache starting. It was time to go.

Ten

When the phone rang late that night I knew it would be Ti, and for the first time in the history of us I felt nervous. Partly because I was worried Mum or Dad would pick up the other line and tell her outright she wasn't to call any more, but mostly because I hadn't decided what to say.

I'd been lying in wait beneath the paper moon on the landing, just in case she called, but I couldn't think how to tell her what had happened with my confession.

'How was school?' she said, trying for casual, at the same time as I blurted out: 'I went to see Kes.'

I could feel the truth set to tumble from me like Lego bricks from Joey's basket, because I had never kept a secret from Ti, and I wasn't intending to start now, but she jumped in before I had finished, and she sounded so shocked that I was embarrassed.

'You really did it? What did he say?'

'He thought I was just making it up because I wanted

my friend back,' I said, amazed at how convincing my lie sounded. Ti's breath was long, and I scrunched my eyes shut and wound the phonecord round my finger, heart bashing at my insides. *He said Chase counts and you don't. That you brought it on yourself. That I should forget you.*

'I mean, he got rid of me pretty fast. I'm sorry, Ti. I feel terrible . . . I should have tried harder. I should have stayed with you when I had the chance or stopped you, or *something . . .*'

'No, I should have stayed with *you* when I had the chance. We never should have gone to that stupid garden.'

The gnawing feeling in my stomach wouldn't go away. I hated knowing things Ti didn't. It made everything uneven between us, like I was an evil overlord and she was some innocent peasant.

'I hate Fairfields without you.'

'I know. I'm going to hate The Bridge without you. Actually I think I'd hate The Bridge *with* you; there's not much to like about it from what Phe says. Soz, I'm not trying to make you feel bad.'

'It's okay. I mean, I know.'

As we embarked on the first awkward silence of our friendship I began to see my dad's point about keeping a phone conversation going for an hour.

'I know who the secret boyfriend is,' Ti said.

'No! Oh my god. Who?'

'Will Fielding.'

'Again?'

'I know.'

'Don't tell anyone. Dad will kill her if he finds out. He caught her sneaking out the window last night.'

Fab had only just forgiven Ophelia for stealing from the till last year. It had never happened before she got involved with Will, and so Fab had banned Ophelia from seeing him. It was kind of funny, because the Fieldings swore it was Ophelia who was the bad influence after they caught Will stealing their car in a late-night attempt to visit her.

Even now Ophelia was only allowed to make the cakes, never to cash up or take money from customers, which maddened Ti because she had to do all the maths, and she was terrible at it.

'Shit! I've messed everything up,' Ti said. 'I mean, I knew it, but I didn't really *know* it. I'm such an idiot! Just another De Furious scratched off the register.'

'Don't say that,' I said. De Furious was a name Alex and Charlie had made up for Ti and Ophelia recently. They said it in this awful Italian accent that was meant to sound like Fab, and it never failed to get a response.

The two of them had been in the café a few weeks ago asking Fab, all innocent, if certain things made him *just de furious* – like when customers got melted cheese on the tablecloth or the wind blew over their sign. They'd nodded along as Fab explained how his customers could do what they wanted so long as they returned to order more

spaghetti, until Ti, seeing what was going on, had 'acciden-
tally' spilled their chocolate milkshake across their laps.

'Charlie must be delighted,' Ti said gloomily.

'She hasn't said anything yet.' I'd lied again. What was
wrong with me? 'You can appeal, though, can't you?'

'I don't know. Dad's not exactly racing to get in front
of the governors again.'

'I hate this,' I said, winding the phone cord between
my fingers. 'What can we do?'

'I don't know. I'm thinking.'

Ti sounded squashed, like she was lying face pressed
to the floor, and I knew she was upside down. I could
picture her in the hallway, with the family of tiny brass
horses and June's Freddie Mercury calendar. She liked
to put her feet against the wall, and rotate so that her
hair trailed off the funny little pouffe they all sat on when
they talked on the phone.

I used to sit there to call Mum and ask if I could stay
the night, back when I was still allowed to ask her things,
and I didn't have any secrets. Those months felt like
years ago, a lovely, easy time that would never return.

'Come over and see me tomorrow? They're playing
table tennis at six.'

'Okay,' I agreed, because I couldn't bear the sadness
in her voice.

I'd done enough lying to Ti for one day. Mum and
Dad would have to take a turn.

Eleven

After delivering Mum's tea and toast and getting Joey installed on his computer, I walked up the hill to Ti's house. I felt bad for lying, but Ti couldn't know that my parents had stopped me from seeing her. She'd always worried they didn't like her, and now wasn't the time for her to discover it was true.

The De Furias' battered black Fiesta wasn't parked in its usual spot by the pavement, so I walked right up to the front door and knocked, praying Ophelia was out too. Ti came to the door.

'He's hidden the damned key!' she shouted through the letter box, and I listened, heart pounding, while she searched for it, cursing her dad energetically.

'I'm sure this is illegal,' she said when she'd finally got the door open.

'They've all gone to Willows and locked me in. Like an actual dog.'

Willows was the local sports centre where Charlie and me used to mess around together while our mums played hockey.

I'd planned to give Ti a big hug, as much for myself as for her, but she stormed into the house before I had chance.

'My appeal failed,' she said, sitting heavily at the kitchen table, and my ears started doing that *wom-wom-wom* thing where you feel sick and dizzy and scared all at the same time.

'It was today?'

'Yeah. No one told me either, until an hour before.'

She wasn't looking at me, which was strange. Had Kes told her I never owned up? Was that why she hadn't given me a hug?

I took the seat beside her, swallowing loudly by mistake.

'Dad's still not talking to me,' she said, shifting in her seat to get comfortable. There was a knock as she banged her knee against the wood, and screaming through her closed mouth, she threw the keys she'd been holding across the room. They clattered against the wall, and I stared at the chip they left in the green paint.

'He won't listen to me! He hates me! Ophelia's the only one in the house being nice to me at all, but *I'm* supposed to be the nice one.'

I walked over to pick her keys up, heart thudding, while she rubbed her hands over her eyes.

'Sorry,' she said, shaking her head, and shutting her eyes, and I wanted to comfort her because I knew how she hated to lose her temper, but what could I say? Her appeal had failed. She was permanently excluded, and here I was sitting in my uniform.

'D'you want a cup of tea?' I said eventually, and she nodded, staring at the plastic seagull fob attached to the house keys. I set about finding what I needed, glad to have cupboards to look into and cups to get. Things were becoming more strained between us, and I couldn't work out how to fix it.

'I thought Dad was going to hit someone he was so mad. He was shouting by the end; I could hear him from outside. They accused him of being a bad parent.'

'Really?'

'That's what he said. Sophie Fielding was worst of all. They shouldn't allow kids' parents on the board; it isn't fair.'

Ti drummed her fingers on the table, while I waited for the kettle to boil.

'It wasn't even about the threat in the end – it was my word against hers so they couldn't throw me out for that – they just made out I was this really horrible student. They pulled out all my marks and detention records and how many times I've been on report. They talked about me wearing black jeans instead of trousers all the time. As if that matters! Everyone wears black jeans! Everyone's in and out of detention. Aren't they?'

She looked to me for confirmation, and I bunched my mouth over to one side because it wasn't strictly true. Seventy per cent of the Fairfields population had probably never spent a day in detention in their lives, and only Ti and a few other kids from the Beacon got away with wearing black jeans instead of proper school trousers. Or didn't get away with it, it seemed.

'I've got to stop thinking about it,' she said. 'It's done. Can I paint your nails?'

She was trying to sound chirpy, and so after setting down our drinks I laid my hands on the butterfly-covered plastic tablecloth. We would pretend this was the recent past, and everything would feel right between us. Ti slipped into beauty-salon mode, asking how I was, and if I was going anywhere nice on holiday this year, then telling me the latest about Will and Ophelia, and how Will had failed his driving test for the second time.

The sweet, toxic smell of the black varnish filled my nostrils, and I watched Ti splay the brush carefully, head low so she could be precise.

'I'm so bored of hearing about him; he's such a brat. His mum and dad are paying for his lessons so it doesn't matter how many times he fails. He actually said that. Can you believe it?'

I could easily believe it. None of the Fieldings worried about money. They owned two hotels on the beach front, as well as the most expensive fish restaurant on the high street, and Sophie had recently opened an organic bakery in the boarded up off-license next door to Fab's café as well. Dad complained about the town getting too fancy, and the locals being priced out, but he'd almost wet himself when he found out Sophie would be selling unleavened spelt bread.

While I blew my nails, Ti scanned the rammed-to-the-rafters fridge. There were Tupperware containers full of leftovers from the café as well as the usual jars of olives and vegetables that the De Furias loved, and I was excited to see what she would bring out. She pulled a foil-covered cake from the middle shelf, and I thought to myself that considering how weird Ophelia was about eating she was brilliant at baking.

This one was soft and caramelly with apple and cinnamon, and Ti cut us each a big slice.

'You can't let the knob jockeys get you down, that's what Ophelia says.'

Ti turned the radio on, beginning the sort of

dancing she knew would make me laugh: A sexy pop starlet plus lobster plus somebody's grandad. Alternating between mouthfuls of sweet cake and bitter tea, I watched her, wishing for the millionth time that other people could see her the way that I did, that she would let them.

And then the front door opened, and my stomach dropped. Ophelia burst in with her headphones on.

'You'd best not be eating my cake!' she shouted, pushing her headphones back to rest round her neck. She laughed in Ti's direction, her whole expression shifting from scary to fun in a nanosecond.

'I shouted again, didn't I? Kept getting funny looks on the bus.'

Her sleek dark hair was parted at the side, so the fringe fell over one eye.

'We only had a tiny bit,' Ti said. 'Please don't be a cow.'

'I'm not talking to you, am I? You can eat as much cake as you like, you're my hero. I'm talking to *this one.*'

Ophelia stared at me, and my cheeks began combusting.

'*She* gets expelled, for something that you did too, and you're round here eating *my* apple cake? In your Fairfields uniform?'

'It wasn't Rosie's fault,' Ti said, while I chewed

frantically, grateful that I had a mouthful of cake, wishing that I hadn't risked a visit.

'Oh? I thought you said she legged it?'

I felt like crawling under the table, but I couldn't move.

'But she owned up,' Ti said. 'I told you, it didn't make a difference.'

'Yeah?' Ophelia said, and I nodded. 'So how come you're not expelled?'

'He didn't believe me.'

'That's convenient,' she said, sizing me up. 'Some people are just born lucky, eh?'

Ti had got up and put her hand on Ophelia's arm, and was pleading with her not to be horrible.

'You don't deserve her,' she said. 'She's a bloody angel. My heroine!' Ophelia kissed Ti's forehead, squeezing her face between her hands, and you would have thought there were eight years between them rather than eight minutes.

She turned away to refill the kettle, water crashing against the bowl, then slammed it back on to its holder, and yanked the fridge door open to find the milk. Everything she did was extra loud, like she overestimated the force needed to move objects.

'You have to remember, Phe, Rosie's mum's ill. She can't have any extra stress at the moment.'

'Pffff!' Ophelia said. 'She just needs to get some

anti-depressants, like Mum did. Take one of them every day, and Bob's your uncle.'

'I'd better go,' I said, because there was no way I could listen again to Ophelia tell me how my mum was just 'a bit depressed'. But neither twin was paying attention to me. Sometimes it was like that when they were together, all their concentration sucked into the other.

'You don't get it, Phe. It's more than that. Anyway, I told you – I got too close. Rosie told me to stay back, and I didn't listen.'

'Bullshit! She just uses her mum as an excuse.'

'Screw you, Ophelia,' I said, slipping my feet into my plimsolls.

'Running away again, are we?' Ophelia said, reaching into the cupboard for the teabags. 'Nice one. Good friend you are.'

'Oh, shut up, would you?' Ti snapped at her, before following me out.

'Thanks for coming over to see me,' she said, as she opened the door, and it was like I was her aunty or a neighbour or something, not her best friend.

'Yeah, thanks for the cake,' I said back. Too much had changed too fast, and I couldn't keep up, and then Ti shut the door, and I hated that she was going back inside to Ophelia who would bad-mouth me all night long.

I wanted the old times back, when Ophelia was

wrapped up with Will, and me and Ti were the sisters, and there wasn't a secret between us. All the way home, I picked Ophelia's apple cake from my molars, stomach churning as though I'd eaten raw chicken, and I wished very badly I had resisted it.

Twelve

It was late when Dad got in from work. He knocked on my bedroom door in his creased-up tweed jacket and jeans, and for a second I thought he knew I'd been to see Ti, but the timid way he pushed my door open told me I wasn't in trouble.

'What now?' I said, continuing to read my camera manual, as he sat on the end of my bed. If he asked me one more time to put myself in Mum's situation I would throw the camera at him.

'I'm sorry you're having a hard time,' he said. 'And I just wanted to remind you that this won't last forever.'

I stopped reading, and looked at him. Why did he have to be so nice?

'You're such a help to me, Rosie, and I know it must be hard, and I just wanted to say thank you for being such a good daughter.'

'I'm not a good daughter,' I said miserably. 'I'm not a good anything.'

'You're a good everything! The way you look after your mum and Joe, I can't thank you enough, Rose. Honestly, I couldn't manage without you. I'm so proud of the way you're handling this.'

Oh god. I couldn't bear it.

'Ti's parents have been locking her in the house like a dog.'

'Oh dear,' Dad said quietly. 'That's not good.'

'But, hey,' I said, 'why stick around when your friends fall on hard times? Better to just move on, find a new crowd, isn't it?'

'*Rosie*,' Dad warned, and I could see how tired he was, how much he didn't need this, but I couldn't stand him being grateful to me.

'No, it's cool,' I said, pretending to read again. 'Who cares about Ti? She's been kicked out of school now anyway. You can congratulate yourself for knowing a bad egg when you see one. And I'll soon forget about her. I mean, I'm just a kid, right? I'm just a teenager. What I want isn't important.'

'Please don't be melodramatic, Rosie,' Dad said. 'We're parenting you, that's all. We want you to make the most of your education, enjoy your time at school. Really, Boo, would it be so bad to get to know some other people? It would be such a weight off if you could just *try*.'

His eyes were so hopeful I could barely look at them. Why couldn't he fly off the handle now and again, like Fab? Give me something to rebel against. But no, he was holding his arms open for a hug, and I needed it just as much as he did, because I was so disappointed in myself, and I couldn't handle him being disappointed in me too.

'Fine,' I said. 'I'll try. If you stop calling me "Boo".'

Thirteen

Grease rehearsals had begun at lunchtimes as well as after school now there were only a few weeks before the end of term, so my hope, as I headed into the canteen was that Charlie, Alex and Mia would be in the Drama block with Chase and all the other theatre minions.

They walked in just as Pat was filling my bowl with chips. Pat was one of the few dinner ladies who'd appreciated the zine Ti and me had made one rainy Wednesday. We'd pushed it under the kitchen door, a little book full of reviews of the school-meal range, with hand-drawn pictures, and it had made her laugh so much she had given us extra food when she served us ever since.

'Long time no see, my sweet,' she said, handing me the overflowing bowl. 'Where's your sister?'

I shrugged, too embarrassed to explain that Ti had been expelled, or that I'd taken to eating a bag of crisps in the toilet cubicle at dinner time.

Waving a note, Charlie made a beeline for the hot food counter, cutting in front of all the kids in the queue with total confidence. Somehow she managed to make school uniform look like it wasn't school uniform. I couldn't work out how she did it. She wore a white shirt and navy jumper and black trousers or skirt like everyone else, but it just looked different.

'We're in the play,' she said to the general area, smiling her sweetest, 'so we're prioritized for dinner. Jacket potato and beans, please. No butter. I hate butter. Butter's *foul*.'

Pat handed her the food she'd asked for, then passed the same to Mia and Alex who had followed with the same requests. Poor them, unable to even enjoy the simple pleasure of butter. The worst thing about seeing them – except for *seeing* them – was that now I couldn't pour gravy (which was free, and therefore extra delicious) on top of my chips. But actually, who cared? They already tormented me, I might as well take the edge off with a nice load of gravy.

'Lot of calories in that,' I heard Charlie say, and so I emptied the jug. Defiantly I picked up a spoon as well as a fork at the cutlery area.

'Blooooooom,' Alex whispered, catching up with me as I pushed my tray to the tills. Charlie laughed too loudly, and the flamethrowers started, and it was so odd how sensitive they made my face. I could feel the air passing over every millimetre of it, and I tried to focus on that sensation, instead of what I might look like, or how humiliating it would be to spill what had become a kind of chip soup.

After you'd paid for your food, there were three steps into the main part of the canteen. One time a Year Seven fell backwards down them on his chair, still holding a forkful of his dinner, and the whole room just came alive with laughter. It *was* funny, especially as the kid was fine, but can you imagine if that was you? The kid still gets called 'chair' today. Like it's his name. Like: '*Oh, hi, Chair. How are you?*'

'*Blooooooom.*'

Alex wasn't letting up, and my bowl and glass juddered a little on my tray. Still I kept my head up like Dad insisted, and looked for a free seat at the end of one of the long tables. The people that designed the layout of school dinner halls definitely didn't remember what teenagers are like. If they did, they would litter single places round the edge of the room, along with tables of twos and threes, instead of these nightmare stretches of twenty-six.

Kiaru and Alisha glanced at me as I stepped down the stairs and I was musing on how they managed to hold their place smack bang in the middle of the school hierarchy when the world tilted and my chip soup began sliding along my tray. I tried to correct it, but my apple juice had tipped over and the sudden pool of liquid made me jump, and then somehow with a roar in my ears, I was sitting down hard, in exactly the way that it was important not to.

'Bloooooom!' went the call, much louder than usual so as to be heard over the cheers and whooping and laughter, and I looked around, with gravy burning my thighs through my tights and hot chips crushed between my fingers to see Charlie, Alex and Mia stood in a line at the top of the stairs, happier than I'd ever seen them – happier than I'd ever seen *anyone* – like my fall was the crowning production of the season. Charlie held her hand out, like she wanted to help me, though she was laughing so hard that she was actually crying, and something came over me, rage I suppose. I took her outstretched hand with my gravied one, and still sitting on the bottom step I gripped for all I was worth, and maybe because she was at the top of the stairs, or because she wasn't expecting it, I managed to pull her down with me.

She fell on to her knees before Alex or Mia could save her, and her jacket potato – no butter – rolled with a slap into my mess of gravy and chips.

The kids standing to get a better look let out a gasp, and Charlie wasn't smiling any more. Alisha crouched beside me now, with her hand on my back, and Kiaru held out a fuzzy-looking grey bundle of toilet roll, like

Granny used to have, and their faces were concerned, the only ones in the whole horror show not gawking.

'Psycho!' Charlie shouted, leaping up as Chase made her way over to us. I wiped my meaty hands unsuccessfully on Kiaru's ball of tissue, and then we were marched to Kes's office where I found myself accusing Charlie of pushing me down the stairs in an on-the-spot explanation of my mad-seeming behaviour.

Unable to tell who was lying, Kes gave us each a week of lunchtime detentions, and though I knew Charlie would probably get a note from Chase to say she was *needed at rehearsals*, I was overflowing with relief. Lunchtime detentions meant my parents would be none the wiser.

'You're going to be sorry for doing that,' Charlie said to me, as we left.

'I don't think I am,' I said, buoyed a little from sticking up for myself. 'I reckon it will always be one of my top five favourite things that I've done.'

'I wonder if it'll always be one of your mum's top five favourite things you've done,' she said drolly, and my feeling of security drained from me. 'Or if maybe she'll get *really stressed*.'

Fourteen

The chips-and-gravy incident didn't help with the 'bloom' call, but people that wouldn't normally smiled at me as I went about the school, and I felt like maybe the gammy leg stump I'd been trailing since Ti had left was healing over a touch. Especially when Alisha found me in the chaos that is the end of the school day, and put her hand on my arm.

'Did you enjoy your dinner?' she asked, and we grinned at each other, as though we were already friends. Alisha wore a smart grey coat with a thick blue scarf wound round her neck, and with her warm hand still on my arm, I felt sort of spectacular. She hadn't spoken to me since Year Seven when she told me my Maths textbook was upside down, but I'd always liked her from afar. She and Kiaru seemed kind and clever, like they knew how to have a good time without hurting anyone.

I thought they were snooty because they wore pretentious glasses, and had houses on Castle Road, but I found them interesting. They arrived at school together every morning in this sleek black four-by-four with tinted windows, and sat at the front of every class. It impressed me the way that they passed notes and sniggered like everyone else, but never got called out by the teachers because they could answer all the questions too.

'*Rosie Bloom*,' she said, and I pressed my lips together, embarrassed by the dumb feeling of pride rushing through me at her attention. When she smiled, her face was even more lovely, her cheekbones high and round, and I felt myself smiling back without choosing to.

'Can you hang out after school?' she said. 'We want to ask you something.'

Linking her wrist through my arm, the way I'd seen her do dozens of times to Kiaru, she led me through the corridors, and outside to the gym, where he was waiting for her.

All the way, she talked about *Grease*, and how she should have been given a bigger part because her singing voice was way better than most of the cast's, and how Pirate FM wanted to do an interview with the 'stars', which was annoying because they were too inarticulate for the radio.

'Sure, they have faces for TV, but none of them should open their mouths!' she moaned, and I laughed but all I could really think about was what she wanted to ask me.

Kiaru lifted his chin in the barest minimum of hello, so I didn't bother smiling. I hoped for a minute to sneak a text to Dad; it was his turn to collect Joey, but he'd worry if I wasn't back by four. Right now I wanted to seem free and easy, and so I just cruised along beside them, as if I often hung out at other kids' houses, rather than going straight home to make sure my mum and brother were okay.

As we walked out the back of the school, seeds and grass stuck to my tights, which still smelled of gravy, and the long grass at the edge of the common whipped my legs. Alisha's breathing was heavy as we marched, but that didn't stop her talking. She laughed at her own jokes, without waiting to see if anyone else found them funny, and I wondered if she didn't notice our lack of response, or didn't care.

Kiaru didn't laugh out loud once, and I realized I hadn't ever seen him do that. Maybe laughing out loud was deeply uncool. I'd have to keep a check on it.

When Alisha ran out of chatter, she sang. She was so uninhibited she reminded me of Ti, except her voice was husky and lovely, while Ti sounded like a punk who'd smoked too many cigarettes. Alisha sang a melancholy Pulp song that Mum played to death up in the attic, and I felt sad, but I didn't want her to stop. Not that she would have, the impression I was getting.

We walked out of town to Castle Road, to where Kiaru, it turned out, lived in the huge white pillared house next door to Charlie Fielding's. I wondered when he'd moved in, and if they bumped into each other a lot, and what he thought of her. He didn't like her enough to give her his granny tissue at least. It was still balled up in my bag, like a memento from a concert, which even I knew was embarrassing.

He led us from the drive round to the back of his house to a huge sloped garden edged with a row of tall Scots pines, through which you could see the ocean. His gate opened out near the cliff path down to Durgan, the same as Charlie's did, and I felt a pang of envy.

Ti thought the Castle Roaders believed the beach belonged more to them than it did to the rest of us because of their gates, and if you saw the Fieldings' summer set-up with deckchairs, Dalmatians, inflatables and barbecues, you might agree. Mum said Ti was jealous, but I'd heard her call Sophie obnoxious when she'd complained about how much money they had to spend maintaining their vintage speedboat.

In the bottom right-hand corner of the lawn, adjacent to the boundary of Charlie's garden, a shed with a glass front overlooked the sea.

'Summer house,' Kiaru said, standing aside so we could enter.

'Can we not just go in the house? It's cold,' Alisha said, but Kiaru ignored her. He put his hair behind his ears.

'Welcome,' he said stiffly when we were all crammed inside.

The walls were covered in drawings of mountains, all peeling at the edges and sun bleached like they'd been up for a hundred years, and the sofa was red faded gingham with patches on the arms, and a patchwork quilt draped over the back. Lowering herself to sit on it, Alisha sent up a puff of dust.

Kiaru gestured for me to take the other side of the sofa, and pulled a beanbag from a corner. It took a while for him to find a dignified position – his legs were too long, and he seemed spiderish in his tight black school trousers and baggy white shirt – and he adjusted the colourful woven bracelets on his left wrist as Alisha teased him for his longness.

Laughing beside me, she was hot as a radiator, and I tried to relax and join in, but I was worried that as soon as she asked me her question my face would go bright red. Her sweet perfume smelt musty from being sprayed and resprayed on to her coat and scarf, and it joined the dust to make my nose itch, and I hoped my first impression wouldn't be blowing snot everywhere in an unprecedentedly powerful sneeze.

'So, Rosie,' Alisha said finally, 'Did your girlfriend

really try to kill Ms Chase? And is she due in court for breaking the rules of her injunction?'

My mood sank. They wanted gossip.

'My *friend*.'

They looked at each other, communicating some-thing important, and I missed that so much, knowing someone well enough you could tell each other things with your eyebrows.

'It's a long story,' I said, and it would have been much easier to make an excuse and head home, but I owed it to Ti to at least try to clear up some of the rumours flying around. Besides, Alisha's black eyes were kind, and still half impressed, and I didn't want to disappoint her.

'That is the weirdest thing I ever heard!' Alisha announced when I got to the revenge poo, and I wondered if I had made an error, but then she started laughing, and Kiaru joined in, and so I carried on, growing more enthusiastic. I told her about our purple balaclava, and Ti using a trampoline to get into Chase's garden, then stepping in the metal dog bowl.

'So *that's* what you do at the weekends,' she said, as though it had been bothering her for a while.

'Used to, we're not allowed to see each other any more.'

Alisha pulled a sad face for one second, but her smile couldn't be suppressed for two. 'So what did you see? Did you discover anything juicy about the secret life of Chase?' Her eyes glittered in anticipation, and I told her about the shadow Ti had seen, and the romantic music, and how that was what had drawn her too close to the house.

'Chase lied about Ti after. She said she threatened her, when she didn't, so I don't know . . . Maybe she did have something to hide . . .'

'How do you know Ti didn't threaten her?' Alisha said.

'Because I was just next door. I heard everything, and Ti would never threaten anyone.' I was lying again – I hadn't heard what happened at all, but I meant it just the same.

'Didn't she punch Charlie Fielding a few weeks ago?' Kiaru said.

'That was Ophelia. And no, she didn't *punch* her. They were practising a routine, and she fell—'

Alisha hooted.

'It's true!' I said automatically, though I wasn't certain myself, in spite of Ti's best efforts to convince me.

'Ti says Chase was stupid, casting like she did,' I said. 'Something was bound to happen.'

'She likes to use natural emotion to get the best performance,' Alisha said. 'That's all.'

'Ophelia ended up getting chucked out of school!'

'That's hardly Ms Chase's fault though, is it? Ophelia needs to learn to hold onto her temper.'

'Ti says Charlie and Mia wound her up.'

'They probably did, but that just makes what Ophelia did even more daft. You can't react to girls like that, it's what they live for . . . Not that Ophelia's much better. It's a shame though, 'cause she's a good actress. She would have been perfect as Rizzo. Much better than that wet lettuce, Mia.'

'As if she'd ever be the leader of a gang!'

'I know. It worked with *West Side Story*, though, didn't it? Chase's approach. Will and Ophelia were dreamy in that.'

'I still don't think it's right, using people's emotions against them, and then throwing them out like pieces of rubbish.' I sounded exactly like Ti.

'That's show business,' Alisha said, and I thought I saw Kiaru rolling his eyes. Was he losing interest in her? Or was it me he found boring?

'She never talks to anyone except for you, you know – Ti,' Alisha said. 'I was her partner in PE once, and she never said a word. I think she's in love with you.'

'She's shy, that's all, and she thinks that—'

'Are Titania and Ophelia *really* their names?' Kiaru interrupted, and something in his voice made me defensive on Ti's behalf.

'Her dad loves Shakespeare,' I said. 'What, d'you think people up the Beacon don't know about him?' Another old line of Ti's.

76

Kiaru looked annoyed, but Alisha put her hand on his arm. 'Finish telling us what happened at Chase's. You said Ti didn't threaten her?'

'No, she didn't, but I ran off, and left her to take all the blame, and then I promised to confess because I felt so guilty, and I thought they might let her back in, if they knew there were two of us, that we were just messing around, but Kes said it wasn't the threat so much as the kind of student she was, and made me think of my family, and told me I should be getting As—'

'He thinks you could get As?' Kiaru said at the same time that Alisha said: 'You realized it was a waste of time.'

'Maybe. Or maybe I just wimped out.'

'You're a good friend to have tried,' she said.

I shook my head. 'A good friend would have confessed.'

'A good friend wouldn't want you to get expelled because they did something asinine,' Kiaru said.

Alisha shrugged, like, *maybe that isn't a bad point,* and I felt worn out all of a sudden, because I had no idea what asinine meant, only that it was something horrible he was assigning to Ti, and as they examined me with intelligent eyes through their tortoiseshell-rimmed glasses, the frames so similar I wondered if they had picked them out together, I felt lonelier and more confused than ever.

Because for so long I'd sworn it was everyone else that was wrong about Ti, but what if it was me?

Fifteen

From: Faerie_Queen666@gmail.com
To: RosieBloomheart@gmail.com
Sent: Friday, 16 March, 16:21:44
Subject: Send help

The Bridge is the worst. The boys are horrible. They run around punching each other in the back of the head and think it's hilarious.

I'm considering shaving my head just to fit in. Do you think I could pull off a skinhead with my gigantic peanut skull? Actually, I could probably cut off my head and nobody would notice. I could drip blood from class to class, neck stump showing, and no one would comment.

What's happening at school? Do you see much of Will? Ophelia thinks he's cheating on her, and asked me to ask you if you'd seen him flirting with other girls. She caught him lying about something and now she doesn't trust him. Around Mia, especially, but also just anyone. She thinks he's irresistible, even to Chase. She's such a bunny boiler, it's embarrassing.

Dad found a love letter when he was washing her jeans. There was no date on it, but he's not convinced it's an old one, and so he's keeping her under even stricter observation. Sometimes I wish she would just get on with it and run away, just to have some peace. She's mean to Mum, and then Dad goes crazy or she's mean to Dad and Mum gets upset. She winds him up on purpose.

Send me a long one back, I miss you. Tell me how your mum is, and how school is, who you are grooming to replace me, any suspicious Chase/Mia/Will behaviour, any bad things that have happened to Charlie Fielding, how much you miss me, how school isn't the same without me, what exactly the importance of getting GCSEs is, and why I shouldn't just top myself now and get this all over with.

Oh, and also AAAAAAAAAARRRRRRRGGGGGGGGHHHHHHH HHHHHHHHHH!

GAGAGAGAGAGAGAGAGAGAGAGAGAGAGAGAGAGAGAGA GAGAGA

MISS YOU. Let's make a plan to see each other. Ophelia thinks she knows where Mum hides the key, so I should be able to get out for a spot of nightwandering soooooon.

Write back.

PS Hug Joey for me

Ti x

From: RosieBloomheart@gmail.com
To: Faerie_Queen666@gmail.com
Sent: Friday, 16 March, 23:55:06
Subject: Re: Send Help

Okay, you asked for it. There have been developments. First the bad news: I fell down Chair's stairs in the school hall. I know, and it was even more embarrassing, because I had a bowl of chips that I'd filled to the brim with gravy, which spilled everywhere, and everyone laughed at me, and then Alex started the 'bloom' call and I honestly thought my head might come off and blood just spout from my neck like a red fountain.

But the good news: my head didn't come off, and I saved the day by pulling Charlie Fielding down with me. She was laughing at the top of the stairs, and I just grabbed her hands, so she could join me sliding around in the soup.

It was pretty much the best thing I've ever done, and I wish I could have videoed it for you and the world. It could be a YouTube sensation.

The next thing, which is more like medium news, is that Alisha Patel and Kiaru Aki helped me in my time of need. (He handed me this ancient bit of loo roll, like my nan used to have, from his sleeve; it was so cute.)

They asked me to join their group for the Drama project so I don't have to do a monologue after all. Hurray! They take school-work really seriously. I don't think anyone's told them it doesn't matter until exams.

Also newsflash: they might not be a couple. Think about it. Have you ever seen them kiss or hold hands or even touch? If they are a couple, I don't think they're into it any more. Kiaru isn't anyway. Alisha might be. She looks at him like she loves him, but he doesn't seem to notice. They're nothing like Ophelia and Will used to be. They're more like my mum and dad or even you and me. Hubba hubba.

Please don't let Ophelia convince you to do anything crazy on her behalf. Honestly, I don't know about Will. He's less cocky since Chase made him director. He walks along beside her with a clipboard, nodding his head and taking notes, with this massive quiff like a Mr Whippy. I see him with Mia quite a lot, but I think it's just for the play. He would flirt with a dustpan and brush (Ophelia does know this, right?) but I'll keep an eye on him, and let you know . . .

Has your dad forgiven you a bit now Ophelia's in trouble again? What happens if you both do something bad at the same time? Don't try it.

I'm sorry that The Bridge sucks. Keep your head down, and you'll be back in a proper school in no time. Maybe even Fairfields? Dream of dreams.

Mum's not good, worse if anything. Her aching is constant, and she's not getting any sleep. Dad's moved to the front room, because of his snoring they say, but I'm scared it's more than that. I heard them arguing last night. Mum thinks Dad doesn't believe that she's ill. It's hard, though. I mean, she looks fine, but she can't *do* anything. Me and Dad never get any rest because we're looking after everyone, and all Mum can talk about is how tired she is.

The house is a tip and Dad only ever gets on at me about it. Joey gets away with everything, because he's little, and everyone feels sorry for him because he's missing his mum. As if I don't miss her too!

Anyway, I'd better go because it's my turn to make the tea. Doctors again Wednesday, hopefully they'll have more of a clue . . .

Keep me posted on the key situation. I want to nightwander with you.

R x

PS Joey has drawn a lion's mane jellyfish for you. Whatever that is.

From: Faerie_Queen666@gmail.com
To: RosieBloomheart@gmail.com
Sent: Saturday, 17 March, 03:55:06
Subject: Re: re: Send Help

Is the gravy story true or did you pull it from my dreams? Rosie, that is the best thing that's ever happened to anyone. Are you sure nobody recorded it? Ophelia did a little bit of wee when I told her she was laughing so much. She says Will's version was quite different . . .

Sorry about your mum. I'll keep my fingers and toes and ears crossed for something useful on Wednesday. Chin up, my lovely.

Mr Whippy! That's it! Ophelia's not impressed, but I am. Next time I see him walk past the café, I'm going to call him that. I can't wait.

You are so dumb. Kiaru likes you! Why else would he have shared his granny roll with you? That's why they've asked you to join their group. It must be. And you like him, don't you? I can tell. Why don't you ever just admit the way you feel? There's nothing wrong with liking someone, you know. There's nothing to be embarrassed about. Wouldn't you want to know if someone liked you? Wouldn't you be pleased? Dad says English people ruin their own lives hiding their feelings, and reading your emails I think he's right . . .

LIVE TRUE, ROSIE BLOOM.

Ti x

Sixteen

Kiaru was dressed in baggy grey jogging bottoms and a white T-shirt, doing something weird on the grass outside the summer house when I arrived, and there was no sign of Alisha, though she was the one that had asked me to go over. I watched Kiaru as he took slow steps barefoot, and made winding, smooth hand movements as though I weren't there. His hair was in a low ponytail.

It had been disconcerting how happy Mum and Dad were when I asked if I could come here, especially when I explained that it was to work.

'Oh, Rosie, that sounds wonderful!' Mum said, and though I pretended to sulk because it wasn't Ti's, really I was excited, and as she pulled me on to the bed with her, laughing, for a minute she was her old self: in bed with a cold or a hangover or needing a nap.

'Capoeira,' Kiaru said, when he finally stopped, and I was surprised to hear he was out of breath. I asked him to spell it. Apparently, sped up, his moves were deadly. Apparently, sped up, it would be quite terrifying. There was no denying he moved nicely, though. Even the way he put on his shoes and threw his shirt over his narrow shoulders was stylish.

'Alisha's ill,' he said. 'Food poisoning. Whole family.'

My pulse rate shot up. What would we talk about? And why hadn't he cancelled? Mum had jumped to the same conclusion as Ti about the whole thing: that he liked me.

'You're a cool girl, after all, and he sounds like a cool boy,' she had said, and as soon as I'd stopped cringing I felt sad that she hadn't called me pretty. Wouldn't that be the regular thing to say? *You're a pretty girl . . .* Would anyone in the world ever think that about me? Mum said it was an unenlightened thing to care about, but I'd heard her getting on at Dad when he didn't compliment her after she'd put on a dress or curled her hair.

Kiaru and me stood on the lawn near the summer house looking at each other, and without Alisha it was awkward. What if he had wanted to cancel but hadn't known my number? Should I offer to leave? He turned and walked to the back door, then lifted the brush mat under an arch draped in yellow roses, and wiped the key he found there on his jogging bottoms. Unlocking the door like it was no big deal, he held it open for me.

Inside the mystery house was nothing like I expected, and I began to understand his reluctance. Magazines piled against the walls and boxes overflowing with various black pieces of technology and winding cables. A huge kitchen, all chrome like you'd see in a restaurant, but without the accompanying gleam. The sink was full of plates and saucepans and there were plastic wrappers all over the sides. Piles of microwave dinner trays.

It was kind of impressive how he didn't apologize for the mess. Maybe it wasn't his mess or he was too proud, or maybe his dad was one of those power parents who drilled their kids with mantras like: Never apologize, never explain.

'Forgot to put the recycling out again. Does it smell bad?' Kiaru asked, which was *almost* an apology. 'We clean, but it's like there's this smell underneath everything I can't get rid of.'

'I can't smell anything,' I lied. 'Toast, surface spray . . .'

It wasn't that it stank, but he was right: there was an unidentifiable dankness underneath the more conventional kitchen smells. My house smelt of garlic and onions from Dad's never-ending supply of pasta, but at least it was recognizable.

Kiaru made pints of tea and buttered a pile of toast, and then I followed him up the stairs, trying hard not to spill my drink though new stains would have been difficult to pick out. Neither of us said anything, but my mind was so busy I hardly noticed. Why was I here if he didn't want to talk? Could he actually like me?

Dust stirred as we climbed the stairs and my nose began to itch.

'Hoover broke,' he said, and I hoped I wouldn't sneeze. Imagine if he thought I'd done it on purpose? As a comment on the cleanliness of his home. I peeked in open doors as we passed – unmade beds, strewn-about clothes, black bags of fabric – each was like the box room that ends up filled with everyone's junk. I'd assumed it would be like Charlie's house, modern and airy, with fresh flowers in vases around the house.

Two flights of stairs and we arrived at an attic room, like Mum and Dad's except you could fit ten of theirs in here. Joey could have skated around it, playing British Bulldogs. Or turned it into a cinema. The whole roof area of the house had been transformed into one beautiful room with eight skylights. After that, it had been rammed to the rafters with crap.

Boxes spilled over with fabrics, and dressmaking models perched on top. Balls of wool and rolls of netting. Fishing rods and keepnets and boxes of tackle. A free-standing bath with wooden legs.

Inside a circle of burnt out tealights stood a gold Buddha statue on a silky sheet, and as Kiaru lit a stick of incense and replaced the candles, I wondered if I was about to become his first human sacrifice.

It wouldn't be the worst place to die. Sunlight shot through the swirling dust in thick lasers, and as Kiaru sat down in a glowing spot I sat with him. It was warm there, the sun dazzling. Lighting the final candle, he looked at me, expectant, and I squinted back.

'I have something to tell you, but first I want you to relax.'

That sounded like a recipe for unrelaxation. Like the opposite of what someone would say if you were going for a massage or something.

'Alisha thinks that you're not a very relaxed person.'

'Okay.'

Was I *supposed* to feel relaxed? *When?* All the time? I'd had no idea. My nose was itchy, and all I could think was how wonderful it would be to really honk it out into a tissue, but Kiaru's intense tone prevented me from asking something as ordinary as where the loo was. Also, if he liked me, I didn't want him thinking about me in relation to the toilet.

'Have you ever tried meditating?' he asked, and I froze. Was he doing a move?

His skin looked firm and smooth, and I hoped the light was having the same effect on me.

'It really helps me think, if I'm stuck or . . . *confused* . . . It clears my mind. Helps me concentrate.'

His expression was endearing as he talked; he seemed really eager to help me.

Did I seem like I needed help?

'D'you want to try?'

'Okay,' I said, and his lips curled in the smallest smile. He took a deep breath in, and then out, and automatically I copied him.

'I find it helps if I close my eyes,' he said, before breathing long and slow again through his nose. The dust was swirling in and out, and I regretted not asking for a tissue before we got started, because the toilet wasn't sexy but neither was blowing mucus across the room at forty miles per hour.

'Pay attention to your breath. Feel it come into your body, the first moment that it hits. Maybe it's the edge of your nostrils or maybe it's higher up. And then out again.'

His voice was deeper than mine, but softer, like he was driving it with his foot only gently on the pedal. I matched my breath to his, trying to ignore the tickle stretching from the deepest darkest part of my nostril to the back of my throat.

'Try not to think about anything: just focus on the feeling of your breath, the way it fills up your lungs. In and out.'

The backs of my eyes tingled. The air coming into my body was thick with fibres and skin flakes and ancient crumbs of crumbs and there was nothing I could do. Kiaru's eyes flew open as I full-body sneezed into the golden air around us.

'Sorry!' I jumped up, face blazing. What must I have looked like just then? Had he seen the mercury filling in my molar? The lumpy back of my tongue? Was he covered in my spit and phlegm and germs?

'It's all right. It's natural. Just a sneeze. Do you want some tissue?'

I nodded, and he reached into his back pocket to take out a soft bundle of the stuff the way he did when I was covered in gravy, and I decided he was the sweetest boy in the world.

'I'm sorry, I was really getting into it. I was trying . . . I just . . .'

Blowing my nose was such a relief that I did it right there, then wished I hadn't.

'God, sorry. I'm not usually this disgusting.'

'You're not disgusting,' Kiaru said matter-of-factly. 'You just worry too much. Do you need more tissue? Do you want to go back outside?'

'I want to finish the meditation.'

Resuming the position, I listened to Kiaru's soft voice, and I thought how odd it was to be here, with him, doing this, and then he reminded me to focus on my breathing, and I did, and then I thought about the way he'd said I wasn't disgusting, and wondered if it meant anything, and I couldn't resist opening my eyes again. I admired his angular face, and narrow boned nose, and then he brought me back to my breathing, and round and round we went like that.

'Okay, last breaths,' he said. 'You're meant to have a little bell that you ring, to come out of meditation, but I don't have one, so you can just open your eyes.'

I blinked, as though I had opened mine at the same time as him.

'It doesn't work straight away. You have to build it, like a muscle. If you keep practising, you'll see. But do you feel more relaxed? I feel more relaxed.'

Kiaru lifted his knees up, looping his arms round them, and his fingers slotted against each other, long and slim, and he was preparing to ask me his question.

'Rosie?'

I nodded, and my face had that oversensitive feeling, and I knew the slightest thing would send it blooming, when every blood vessel seemed to tingle with anticipation of looming embarrassment.

'Okay, so . . . the question . . . Alisha hasn't really got food poisoning . . .'

There was a kind of pressure building in the room, and my stomach dipped like I'd gone over a bump in the car.

'And this might sound dumb.' He was looking at me very intensely, and my blood pumped at an alarming rate. Mum and Ti were right!

'But . . . she really likes you.'

My heart did a double take.

'I mean, she's sort of *in love* with you.'

She was sort of *in love* with me. *She* was sort of *in love* with *me*?

Kiaru looked at me, excited to hear what I would say, but I was pre-language.

'So . . . ?' he said, in the same tone I'd heard dozens of times in the dinner hall as kids confessed their friends' feelings to each other.

Disappointment was like gaining a hundred stone. I was heavy enough to fall through the attic floor.

His brown eyes were so pretty.

'So you and Alisha *aren't* a couple,' I said, almost to myself.

'No. And you aren't . . . Ti really wasn't . . . You weren't . . .'

I wanted to twist down into the earth like a drill, and never be seen again.

'She was *so* sure you were in the closet.'

'Is that why you wanted to be friends? *She* wanted to be friends,' I corrected, and I couldn't keep the sadness from my voice.

Kiaru said no, but he didn't meet my eye. Silence yawned around us, and now it was awkward, deeply awkward, because how much had my disappointment shown? It must have been all over my face when he was telling me. I fiddled with a splinter sticking up from the floor for a few seconds, then stood, realizing Kiaru wasn't going to say anything else. For him, the point of the day, and me being there, was over.

'Tell her I'm sorry. I hope I didn't lead her on,' I said, and then I did what I was best at.

I ran away.

Seventeen

Sunday afternoon Joey begged me to go with him and Dad to the aquarium, but I couldn't face it. All those creatures in their tanks, what was the point? I went upstairs to lie with Mum instead. She had new music to play me, so we spent hours listening together.

Thinking over the time I'd spent with Kiaru and Alisha, I felt embarrassed. Had I led Alisha on? I tried to think of everything I'd said and done, but it was hard to understand how you came across from inside yourself.

Maybe it was because I blushed when she talked to me. Or because I laughed at her jokes. But I was just trying to be friendly. I laughed at Ti's jokes too. I was an easy laugher! Really, though, what had she seen in me? Beneath the blushing and the nerves and my puppy fat, had I got . . . *something*?

Mum found a dim-witted new series about Californian rich kids for us to watch, and I ate the latest grapes Dad had bought, ignoring the looks Mum was shooting at me. She knew something was wrong, but it wasn't her style to push. She'd told me she was feeling down, hoping to draw a confession, but I resisted. My problems were small compared to hers, that's what I had to remember. Dad didn't even have to say it any more. I'd seen the headaches come when she got upset.

I popped grapes in my mouth until Mum put them out of reach, worried about my digestion. I was desperate to talk to Ti, but how could I explain my fear of having no friends again when she'd been forced to attend The Bridge?

The all-American girls on the telly were neat and polished and attractive. It was the same way Alisha was attractive, in a manicured, careful way that took hours behind doors. It was nice – but could I *like* her? Could I kiss her and hold her hand and . . . I shook my head without meaning to, and Mum asked me what was up again, and I wanted so badly to tell her, to let her help, because she was wise, and open, and what harm could it do?

But then a gorgeous girl with lush auburn hair and expert make-up kissed a beautiful black-haired boy and I thought of Kiaru, and my nerves pinged, not because he was a boy, but because kissing *him* made sense. I could imagine it. I could imagine it so well. My eyes closed, then flew open, remembering I was lying beside my mum. I prayed I hadn't sighed or anything, and as the screen kiss

95

dragged on I had to work really hard not to fidget until, finally, the shot changed. Mum let out a breath and I realized I'd been holding my breath too.

Maybe we weren't ready to talk about any potential lesbianism just yet.

The black-haired boy got on a motorbike and he was nothing like Kiaru really, except the way he put one hand in his back pocket.

Of course, he wasn't interested in a girl like me! He probably wasn't interested in any of the girls at our school. He probably liked older girls who knew what capoeira was and didn't blush at the sound of their own name. He probably liked girls that had faces for television, girls like Charlie Fielding or Mia Lewis like every other boy in our year.

Charlie was his girl next door. Literally. The thought made my stomach roil with anxiety. How had he managed to escape the notice of the popular girls? And when were they going to claim him?

On screen the scenic fake-teen girls talked about being friends forever, and the thought of Monday at school heavied my stomach. When Alisha found out I wasn't in the closet, would she stop talking to me? Would they let me finish the project with them, or was I back to doing a one-woman show?

'Fidgeting hell, Rose. Can you stay in one position? I feel like I'm on a boat.'

'I don't feel well.'

Mum's tone changed, and she shifted position so her hand could reach my forehead. 'What's the matter, baby? You don't feel hot.'

'I feel sick,' I said in a small voice. Usually I told her off for calling me 'baby'.

'Do you feel sick or do you need to be sick?' she said carefully, because as a kid, I used to have a problem recognizing the difference, resulting in gross carpets and car mats and on one occasion, a gross granny's handbag.

'I just need to lie still,' I said, and after checking I was absolutely certain I wasn't going to blow, Mum did what I had hoped she would. Lying just behind me she drew her cool hand over my forehead, until I began to calm a little.

'Is everything okay, Boo?' she said. 'Did something happen at your new friend's house?'

I closed my eyes.

'You can talk to me. You know that don't you?' she said. 'I miss our talks.'

There was a burning sensation in my nose because I missed our talks too, but I was so scared of getting it wrong again that I just gave her a cuddle and breathed in her smell, and it was almost, almost enough.

Eighteen

On Monday morning, after an awkward hello in our form room, Alisha linked my arm to walk to Drama. Kiaru strode off ahead, so it was just the two of us, and I wondered if they'd planned this or if he was naturally considerate. Alex and Charlie passed with their arms round each other, Mia tagging along at the side, tugging her too-short skirt down as she walked. Her legs were amazing, perfectly proportioned with lovely slender ankles.

Still it looked annoying, wearing a short skirt like that; trousers were more comfortable for sure. Mia always looked self-conscious. You could imagine her straight after school, taking off her tight shirt and short skirt, and putting on the biggest, baggiest pyjamas she could find. The three of them melted into the mass of navy-blue-clad kids making their way to first lesson.

'I hope you aren't offended that I thought you were a lesbian,' Alisha said quietly, and I shook my head violently.

We were going to discuss it? I'd assumed it would be this huge elephant following us around the school until we sat our GCSEs, and here she was just pulling me up on to its saddle with her. What new world was this?

'It was just something about you . . . you know. You don't wear make-up, and you leave your hair nice and natural, and you always wear oversized shirts and jumpers and pumps. And then you and Ti seemed basically married . . .'

'I wasn't offended,' I said honestly. 'It was . . . nice. It was just . . . unexpected.'

'I hope it hasn't weirded you out. I really do want to be friends.'

'Me too!'

'And I don't want you to think I'm ashamed, because I'm not. I'm so not, it's untrue. It's just my mum is religious, and my sister's still in sixth form, and so . . . I can't really parade it. *Yet.*'

'Okay.'

'But I'm not going to be all lovesick over you or anything, I promise. I want a girlfriend. Like, an actual 100% lesbian who wants to lick my bits and everything. You know? I'm ready. I'm going to make it happen.'

I nodded, impressed, and again I thought of Ti. Her and Alisha would probably hit it off, if they ever got the chance to talk properly.

It was a nice walk on a clear day like today, because the

Drama block was set a little apart from the rest of school, and so you had to cross the playing fields, and beyond those the common's long grass rippled in the wind.

Kiaru was up ahead, with the rest of the class, waiting for Chase to come and unlock the building, and I noticed that he stood near Charlie and Alex, nodding at something Charlie said. I felt a spike of jealousy dig in between my shoulder blades.

'How about Ti?' Alisha said, and I tried to recall what she'd been saying. 'Is she gay?' she prompted, impatiently, and I realized it had never occurred to me. I assumed she liked boys, but she'd never really talked about it.

'You don't know?' Alisha said, leaping on my pause. 'Well, think about it. Has she ever fancied anyone? Does she talk about boys from school? Because if she doesn't, maybe she's like me. Or maybe she really is in love with you . . .'

'Nooo,' I said, drawing the word out as though the idea was silly. What a strange thought. I pushed it away. Ms Chase's vintage high heels clicked on the path behind us, late as usual, and Kiaru was smiling at Charlie now. She bent her head forward and laughed, and my stomach rolled. Alex looked unclear on what was so amusing.

'Did you think it was Kiaru that liked you?' Alisha whispered, following my gaze, and I looked at the tarmac so my hair would hide my face.

'Oh, Rosie, you're so adorable,' Alisha whispered. 'If only you could see yourself.'

'I should have thought about that,' she said, sadly.

'Sorry, sorry, sorry!' Chase trilled unapologetically, overtaking us. She sounded so fake as she greeted her favourites, and I wondered if she was ever genuine. Maybe if you devoted your whole life to pretending, you forgot how to tell the difference between truth and lies. Maybe you spent the whole time in character.

Since Charlie got cast as Sandra Dee, she'd started wearing a red ribbon around her ponytail, and looking around wide-eyed, like she was shocked by everyday things like insults and wedgies and swearing.

Kiaru had pulled an extra seat over to their double table, and I placed my bag there shyly. Chase didn't notice the new arrangement. There were only two weeks until show night, and some of her 'stars' were in this class, which made the rest of us invisible.

She opened a list of questions on the projector, and told us to get on with it, then went to sit with Charlie, Alex and Mia, talking intently as though plotting to save the world. The whole class started chatting, catching up about the weekend and who fancied who. Drama in the last weeks of term was a total doss. It was why me and Ti had taken it.

'So, we still need to work on our Drama project,' Kiaru said, and Alisha started laughing.

'Yeah, what is it?' I said, confused, and Alisha nudged me with her shoulder.

'Silly, it was you.'

Kiaru smiled, and a warm volt of contentment spread through me: I had a force field again.

Alisha was listing every single famous and non-famous female she fancied when Will arrived in class. Chase waved him over, and he pulled up a seat with the chosen ones, vanilla hair flicked up like a Mr Whippy. I whispered his new name, and Kiaru laughed out loud for once, which sent a flush of glee through me.

Will pretended not to notice the girls elbowing each other. He was used to it by now. He played guitar and wrote his own songs, and when he occasionally busked on the pier girls from school would set up camp around him, singing along as though he were already famous. Everyone had been surprised when he asked Ophelia out because he was like a healthy clean-cut boy-band member, and she was the kind of teenage girl that scorns cheesy boy bands.

Kiaru and Alisha were confused when Will waved to me, and I explained how we'd played together when we were little, when I was still friends with Charlie, and then, seeing how interested they were, I told them about him and Ophelia reuniting and her suspicions about Chase, and they agreed to help me spy on him.

'I'll tell you if he takes any other girls back to his house,' Kiaru said.

'And I'll flirt with him at rehearsal,' Alisha said. 'Test his resolve.'

By rights, Alisha should have been sitting with the chosen ones, seeing as she had a speaking part – she was the annoying preppy girl who befriended Sandy at the start of the story – but Chase hadn't invited her to sit with them, and we could tell it stung. Because she told us, every three minutes.

She threw herself into watching Will instead, and I began to feel uneasy. Ophelia and Will were supposed to be a secret after all, and Fab would go all Godfather if he found out.

We watched as the cast listened rapt to Chase's advice about singing and controlling nerves, and it was hard to miss the way Will looked at her. The word 'enthralled' wasn't enough, and I wrote it on Alisha's Drama book in capital letters.

Alisha underlined it about ten times. Kiaru drew lines coming off it, and an exclamation mark after, as though it were being shouted.

Will was talking now, something about authenticity and expressing maximum personality onstage, and we watched for Chase's response, but she barely looked at him, choosing that moment to scan her noisy class instead. We ducked our heads, pretending to work.

PLAYING HARD TO GET, Kiaru wrote when we felt her attention leave us.

A few minutes later, Will pointed to a note on his clipboard, and his finger brushed Chase's as she leaned in to look. Alisha bashed her thigh against mine.

UNNECESSARY BODY CONTACT!!!!! she wrote. *THAT'S WHAT I DID TO TEST YOU. (YOU LOVED IT.)*

I guffawed by mistake, and Chase's attention hurtled towards us. Coughing, I stared earnestly at the whiteboard, then scribbled in my book. I mouthed the words of one of the questions to myself, frowning as though I were trying to get to grips with it.

Consider how character can be revealed through action.

Me darting through the gap in Chase's fence leapt into my mind. I pictured myself preparing Mum's breakfast tray this morning instead.

Chase returned to her avid cast.

GUILTY! Alisha wrote.

At break time Kiaru told me that Alisha had shifted her attentions to a tall, confident girl with purple hair called Ava Berry.

'She falls in love a lot,' he admitted, as we watched her beaming at Ava in line for the tuck shop. I felt a pang of something like foolishness or disappointment, but it vanished as quickly as it came because Kiaru leaned in to whisper in my ear, and his breath there sent a shiver all the way down my back.

'There go the lovers,' he said, and Will walked past the canteen with Chase. He handed a pile of books to her, and we watched as he laughed at something she said, before handing her a piece of paper. He looked at her in a slightly mooning way, and she smiled wide, and it looked for a second like maybe something really was going on between them.

As if sensing our scrutiny, Chase looked around. She dismissed Will with a curt nod, but the change only made it seem more suspicious. Scanning the books he'd left behind, with the piece of paper in her hand, she seemed overly aware of her visibility. It was a feeling I was familiar with, and I recognized it in the way that she held herself. Kiaru dug his elbow into my side, and I returned the motion, and we went back and forth like that, delighted with this new piece of evidence of the affair.

'A love letter!' I said.

It wasn't until afterwards that I felt guilty.

The thrill of Kiaru's elbow pressed against me had made me forget what an affair between Will and Chase would mean for Ti. Ophelia would be heartbroken if Will cheated with anyone, but she'd be suicidal if it was with Chase. And Ti had sworn me to secrecy. What was I thinking blurting it out to Kiaru and Alisha like it was all a game?

From: Faerie_Queen666@gmail.com

To: RosieBloomheart@gmail.com

Sent: Wednesday, 21 March, 08:42:16

Subject: Re: re: Warfare

You're totally gay! At least we know now, and you won't have to spend your whole life in the closet. Tell Joey I can't wait to see the jellyfish. Lion's manes are the best. Maybe you can bring it to the café on Saturday? Mum got Dad to agree that if you pop by, I can have my lunch break with you. We can have the good batch of Parmigiana, before it all goes . . . Plus we've got that fancy lemonade in that you like.

Some brute punched me in the back of the head at school today. This horrible tall boy called Leon Woodhouse just walked up behind me and *wham*. He has a ratty moustache and lips that are always wet. I just want to wipe his mouth for him. How hard can it be? It wasn't that bad a whack, but still. WTF? Everyone thought it was really funny, like this clever prank. God. So yeah. I now have a lump the size of an egg on the back of my head.

Ophelia thinks it's really funny and will only call me Egghead. The good thing is that it's made the olds feel sorry for me. Even Dad. He's definitely softening. He made me coffee this morning for the first time in ages.

My counsellor (never thought I'd have to write that) says my chances of getting back into a mainstream school are good. I mean, I'm easily the best behaved kid at The Bridge. I ignore everything and everyone and just get on with my work, even Geography. I wish I'd tried harder at Fairfields. I thought you had to do something really bad to be expelled, like Ophelia did. I didn't know they could throw you out for not trying hard enough.

It's strange having lunch and walking around and sitting in lessons without you to talk to. I'd forgotten what it's like not having a best friend. How you have to save up all your jokes and hold your laughter in all the time. I keep looking around to tell you stuff. Maybe I'll get a notebook, and then you can read it . . . *Notes from The Bridge.*

Erm, Ophelia's eight *minutes* older than me. And what gave you the impression that she would ever take the blame for anything? I get in trouble because of her more likely. When Ophelia tried to run off with the till money Dad stopped talking to me for a month because he didn't believe I hadn't known what she was planning.

And help with cleaning? She won't even do the bathroom once a month when it's her turn. I end up doing it because otherwise Mum does, and then we get a bollocking off Dad. Learning how to be from an 'older' sister like Ophelia isn't the best recipe for success. See *Notes from The Bridge.* Have you even been reading my emails?????

Sorry to hear about your mum. Is she really getting worse? What did the doctor say? Your dad will move back upstairs soon; it probably is just his snoring. My dad sleeps on the settee all the time. I think it must be normal.

He says I can have my break any time between twelve and two, and I can have ninety minutes!

Can't wait to see your silly face.

Titania 'Egghead' Esquire

From: RosieBloomheart@gmail.com
To: Faerie_Queen666@gmail.com
Sent: Thursday, 22 March, 21:33:52
Subject: Re: re: re: Warfare

Oh no! Your poor head! Did you tell the teacher? What a dick Liam Woodhouse is . . .

I'm so sorry but I don't think Saturday is going to work. Mum came downstairs yesterday (this is a big deal) cos she had to go to the doctors, and when she saw the state of the house she actually fainted. Bit melodramatic, I thought. Not really, I was scared. Obviously it wasn't the state of the house, but she's that weak these days. I don't know why I'm joking about it.

Anyway Saturday is now pegged as The Big Clean. I asked Dad if I could nip out just for lunch, and he started guilt-tripping me. Saying he knows he relies on me too much, but can I just help him out a little bit longer? I couldn't say no. I'm so sorry! : (

Maybe next Saturday?

The good news is we have a diagnosis. Chronic fatigue syndrome. Not that good news really, but Mum's relieved to have an explanation. She's got some drugs that might help, but the doctor says it's trial and error, so she might get worse before she gets better, if you know what I mean. But she might get better! I might get my mum back! I am gonna row with her so much!!!

Funny that you're working harder. I'm working harder too. Alisha and Kiaru don't like to talk while the teacher's talking or mess around or anything like that, except for Drama, which isn't a real lesson anyway. They'll probably still get A*s. They're super square, nowhere near as much fun as you.

Alisha likes Ava Berry now. She's bought pink hair dye, hoping that will impress her, and is building up the courage to ask her out.

True or false? Charlie and Alex did the routine for 'You're the One that I Want' at the bus stop yesterday. True! Still cringing.

Okay, and don't tell Ophelia because it might not mean anything but I saw Mr Whippy hand Chase a note yesterday. Inappropriate? Will keep you posted.

Sad and sorry about Saturday.

Roseroony xxxxxxxxxxxxxxxxxxxxxxxxxxxxxxxx

From: Faerie_Queen666@gmail.com
To: RosieBloomheart@gmail.com
Sent: Thursday, 22 March, 21:40:41
Subject: Re: re: re: re: Warfare
NOOOOOOOOOOOOOOOOOOOOOOOOOOOOO!

How can this be happening? Why is everyone conspiring against us? Did you tell your dad about the Parmigiana? Mum says she'll stretch to portions for all the family, if it will stop me moping . . .

Titanic Parsnips xx

Nineteen

The truth was that I wasn't allowed to go to the De Furia café on Saturday. I'd begged and pleaded with Dad, but he'd flat-out refused.

'We said no Titania until she sorts herself out,' he said. 'You'll stay in and clean the house like you promised. You might not realize it yet, but it's important to make good on your word.'

I told him he was as bad as Fab, working me like a slave on a Saturday when everyone else was out with their friends, but he only laughed and called me a brat.

'I'm being punished because Mum's got CFS. As if her being ill isn't bad enough!'

'Please don't be melodramatic, Rosie. It's one Saturday,' he said, but I could tell I'd hit a nerve.

The doorbell went as I was pulling ancient pickle jars from the fridge, and I was delighted to see Alisha and

112

Ava with their best smiles and good girl demeanour at the door. Dad shook their hands with his pink marigolds, and complimented their colourful hair.

'You must have very liberal parents,' he said, and Ava laughed.

'They're total bohemians,' she said. 'They reckon I can't do anything worse than they did.'

I could almost hear Dad's sigh of joy at that. There was nothing he loved more than bohemians. If it was up to him, we would be home-schooled and barefoot. We probably wouldn't even wear clothes.

'They're letting me have a fancy-dress party for the end of term,' she said. 'So we're going shopping for costumes, and we just wanted to ask: can Rosie come?'

How impressive Ava seemed, and how unfair it would be if he said yes to her when he wouldn't say yes to Ti. How absolutely I would forgive him if it meant I could go outside.

'Just for a couple of hours, Dad. *Please.* I'll work extra fast when I get back, and I'll do all the worst jobs. I'll even wash out the recycling bin.'

Ava and Alisha smiled angelically.

'Oh *go on then*,' Dad said, and I leapt up from the fridge, dumping a mouldy jar of jalapeños in the sink and pulling off my gloves. 'But back for one, I want us all to eat together, your mum too.'

'Yes! You're the best! Thank you! I'll be two minutes. Just let me get changed.'

As I searched for my blue and black checked shirt, I could hear Alisha and Ava charming my dad in a double whammy tag team of well-brought-up-ness, and I thought of how awkward Ti always was when she came round.

I kissed Dad's cheek and promised Joey, who was clinging to me and whining as I tied the laces of my plimsolls, a present from the charity shop.

'Don't worry about us,' I heard Dad shout like he was falling down a canyon as I closed the door. 'We'll be dust-i-n-g!'

Alisha was practically swooning with pride as we left, and as she linked arms with Ava I wondered if she had worked up the courage to tell her how she felt. Ava shrugged as we complimented her on winning my dad over.

'You were so convincing! You should be a politician,' Alisha gushed.

'His hair is exactly the same as my dad's. He likes Pulp, right?'

Alisha beamed at me, as I admitted my dad was a huge Jarvis Cocker fan, and I tried to smile back, but now the pleasure of escaping was fading, a guilty feeling about Ti was rising up.

Seagulls hounded for scraps overhead, and I reminded

myself that I hadn't lied on purpose, that I *was* supposed to be cleaning. Still, that wouldn't make a difference if I bumped into her.

The De Furia café was on Dove Lane, just off the main high street. It used to be one of the only shops not boarded up, but now it was the scruffiest-looking place on the road. Since she took over the premises last month, Sophie and Fab were at war. Sophie said Fab's regulars smoking in their shared doorway brought the tone of the area down, and Fab said it was none of her bloody business.

He and Ophelia flicked their cigarette stubs in her bakery's direction whenever they could get away with it.

Dove Lane was away from all the charity shops, so there was no reason I would see Ti, since she was working, but what an alien thing to think. When had I ever not wanted to bump into Titania?

Ava pooh-poohed my suggestion to go into the costume shop, and Lettie sided with her.

'They only have ready-made stuff,' Ava said, as if that explained it, and I felt a twinge of embarrassment because I hadn't known that ready-made meant worse. A Saturday not long ago, Ti and me had spent her whole lunch break there, becoming pirates and superheroes and sailors. We'd sworn to save forty pounds each and buy matching mermaid outfits so that we could wear them to school the next non-uniform day, but Ti had got chucked out before we had chance.

The dress had fanned out into a sparkly tail at the bottom that wiggled when you walked, and I wondered what I was doing with these girls that couldn't appreciate such a thing when Ti was just around the corner.

And then I spotted Kiaru.

Standing by the phone box on the pier he wore tight jeans and a huge parka, though it was much too warm, with white canvas pumps. His hair was getting even longer, and it looked so cool in a centre parting tucked behind his ears as he stood waiting for us.

Alisha hugged him, and I wished I was like her, able to give people hugs without seeming awkward or desperate, but I was still only just managing to keep my head up when I spoke. Kiaru's face broke into a smile as he pointed out an ancient couple in matching raincoats like it was the cutest thing ever, which it was. Was he being this adorable on purpose?

Alisha linked my arm, and we walked into the animal shelter charity shop, and maybe Mum was on to something when she said it felt different to be part of a group. We tried on hats and wigs and glasses for each other and considered options for costumes: dinner ladies? OAPs? Monsters? Witches? Wizards? Cats?

Charlie and Mia were outside the milkshake shop, and they sniggered as they saw us leaving, but we didn't care.

'They're just jealous because we're fabulous and happy,' Ava said, and I wondered if maybe she was *too* confident, because the word fabulous always made me cringe. If Ti was here, we would be nudging each other, but I didn't know anyone well enough for that. I scoured the racks for something that might make Kiaru laugh.

'They're not good people,' Alisha said, holding a baby blue woolly cardigan for Ava's approval. 'But they're popular anyway.'

'No one *actually* likes them, though,' Ava said. 'Do they know that?'

'Chase doesn't help by giving them the starring roles,' I said.

'It makes more people want to be in the show, though,' Alisha said. 'That's why she does it. Hardly anyone used to audition before she started casting the popular kids. Remember, Ki? I played Princess Jasmine in Year Seven,' Alisha said, and Ava began gushing about how much she would have loved to see that.

It was true that Chase had persuaded Ophelia to audition last year, but I hadn't really thought about why. Ophelia was so much more interested in dodging lessons and smoking, that Chase had almost had to kidnap her, but she must have been impressed because she cast her as the female lead in *West Side Story*, opposite Will.

'We had to do two performances last year, because so

117

many people wanted to see the play,' Alisha said. 'System works.'

'System's rigged,' I said, and I sounded so much like my dad that I pressed my lips together, afraid of what I'd come out with next.

I dug through a basket of accessories while Ava and Alisha scanned the shoes.

Kiaru held up a white doctor's coat. 'Scientists?'

'We could be crazed doctors,' Ava said. 'We could douse it in blood.'

'Ava, why do you always want to douse everything in blood?'

Alisha's face looked as though it might split open from smiling, and the way Ava looked back at her, I knew she had got up the courage to ask.

I was listening to Ava explain why Shake it Till You Make It's peanut-butter-banana was superior to their flake-caramel when I saw her out of the corner of my eye.

Titania.

With her curly hair bunched up in a net and tomato sauce down her black-and-white-checked work shirt, she had the blank expression of someone in their own world, and realizing she hadn't seen me I dodged into the milkshake shop.

My cheeks flamed, and I must have looked like a real

buffoon, but the kid behind the counter was wearing a straw boater, so I let myself off.

'Rosie?'

At the sound of her voice I was instantly out of breath. The boater watched us like we were an al fresco performance of *A Midsummer Night's Dream*, and I wished for an invisibility cloak or just to be more skilled at being a person.

'Thought you were spring-cleaning.'

Ti looked angry, but her tone gave away her hurt, and I knew I couldn't explain. With her hair pulled back tight, hands on her hips, she was just like Ophelia.

'D-dad let me off. He said I can do my bit later. He reckoned it could be the last sunny day for a while,' I stammered.

Ti blinked, and I could almost hear her thinking: *So why didn't you come and see me?* I felt so awful.

Kiaru, Alisha and Ava were now in the shop too. Kiaru turned his attention to the board, and Alisha followed his example, squeezing Ava's hand so she would stop staring.

Ti's eyes were accusing, and I wanted to make it all right, but what could I say? How would I have felt if I'd caught Ti dodging into a shop so she didn't have to talk to me? It wasn't imaginable. Ti would never do it.

I felt so ashamed I wanted to cry, but everyone was looking at me and I couldn't think of any words. Then, for some reason, Ava stepped in.

'It was my fault,' she said. 'I talked her dad into letting her come out. I needed help with something. She really was supposed to stay in.'

'So your dad didn't want you to come?' Ti said quietly, without acknowledging Ava or anyone, only me, and Alisha was right – it was weird how she did that. She was so intense, that was the problem. She never skated over things or made them easy. Alisha or Ava would probably just have walked by the shop, pretended they hadn't noticed me, that they weren't hurt. But Ti always had to confront everything.

'It wasn't like that,' I lied, and the way Ti looked at me then, like I was even more pathetic than she'd thought, because I was caught and still lying, made me want to blend my head in the shake-maker.

'*There* you are!' Ophelia shouted, stepping into the shop. She had her headphones on as usual, and was holding two carrier bags full of ciabattas. 'Where the hell's the squid?'

'I didn't get it yet.'

Ophelia noticed me, and then Kiaru, Ava and Alisha. 'These your new mates then? Sacked off Ti, have you?' she asked, and I felt my cheeks combusting.

Ava frowned at Ophelia, like she was ridiculous, and I wanted to reach over and uncrease her face.

'We're just getting a milkshake,' I said.

'*Cool*,' Ophelia said, like it was the most deeply tragic endeavour in the world.

120

'I'll call into the café later,' I said to Ti. 'I was going to come and say hi anyway. After . . .'

'Lunch is over,' Ti said. 'Don't worry about it.'

For some reason Ava and Alisha had got an attack of the giggles, and were doing a terrible job of hiding it. They covered their mouths, shoulders shaking, the way Ti and me used to just before Ms Chase had enough and kicked one or other of us out of Drama.

Ophelia stepped forward fast.

'Are you a clown?' she said, and Ava took a step back, pressing against the wall, face suddenly serious beneath her short purple hair. 'Because you look like a clown.'

After a few seconds, Ophelia stepped back, and walked casually to the door and I wondered if her heart was racing like mine, but she looked perfectly unruffled. Ti's face as she looked around at all of us was unreadable, the way she made it for teachers and customers she didn't like.

'Don't come by the café again,' Ophelia said, pointing at me. 'You're not welcome. Come on, Ti.'

Ti followed her sister out of the shop, without looking back at me, and my hands were shaking. Kiaru put his hand on my back, and Alisha put her arm round Ava who looked bewildered.

It was the kid with the boater who broke the silence.

'Ophelia De Furia is *hot*.'

From: RosieBloomheart@gmail.com

To: Faerie_Queen666@gmail.com

Sent: Saturday, 24 March, 13:32:11

Subject: SORRY

Ti, I'm so sorry about today. It wasn't as bad as it looked. Please let me try to explain. I should have said more in the shop, but I couldn't think. My mind went blank because I felt so bad . . .

Today really was The Big Clean, but Ava and Alisha turned up and convinced my dad to let me out, and I was going to come to the café, I've been missing you so much, and I really wanted to see you, and then Kiaru turned up, and I know it's pathetic but I just sort of went along with them because he was there, and you were right, I do like him, I like him so much, and I haven't seen your mum and dad since everything happened, and, God, I'm the worst. I know it. You can't make me feel any worse about myself than I already do. Your sister's right to hate me.

I really want to make it up to you, Ti. To show you what a good friend I can be. Please. Everything's got so weird lately, and all I want is for us to get back to normal.

Please, please, please forgive me. You're my best friend in the world, and I love you. : (

R xxxxxxxxxxxxxxxxxxxxxxxxxxxxxxxxxxxxxxxxxxxxxxxxxxxxxxxx xxxxx

From: RosieBloomheart@gmail.com
To: Faerie_Queen666@gmail.com
Sent: Saturday, 24 March, 14:04:19
Subject: PLEASE TALK TO ME
Please talk to me, Ti. I know I don't deserve it, but I'm miserable.

I don't know what I'd do if I lost you.

: (

From: RosieBloomheart@gmail.com
To: Faerie_Queen666@gmail.com
Sent: Saturday, 24 March, 15:05:59
Subject: PLEEEEEEEAAAASSSE

Ti, I mean it, I'm so sorry. At least just let me know you got my email. I rang, but Ophelia keeps hanging up. Tell me what I can do to make it up to you.

Please reply. I need to hear from you. I couldn't face it if we weren't best friends any more.

Can you sneak a phone call? Or sneak out? Or just reply on here? Please.

PLEASE.

Just reply saying you've got these, even if you're not ready to talk, and I'll leave you alone.

xxxxxxxxxxxxxxxxxxxx <3 <3 <3 : (<3 <3 <3 xxxxxxxxxxxx xxxxxxx

From: RosieBloomheart@gmail.com
To: Faerie_Queen666@gmail.com
Sent: Saturday, 24 March, 16:01:08
Subject: ; _ ;

I'm really sorry for any times I took ages getting back. It feels horrible. It must have been rubbish moving to a new school and then having me abandon you too. You must hate me. You must be feeling really sad and cross. I can't explain it, but I feel horrible. Sad face and soul.

You will always be my best friend, even if I'm not yours.

Love,

Rosie x

Twenty

Saturday night, after hours of punishing myself for being so selfish, Ti solved my problem for me. There was a banging noise while I was relistening to Mum's new music on my bed, but I thought it was the drums, then a different song came on, and I could still hear it.

Thunk.

I took my headphones off, and went to my side window. Standing on the drive, with her hair piled on top of her head in a messy bun: Titania.

Beside her, pushing sleek dark hair back from her face, smoking a cigarette: Ophelia.

Both were dressed head to toe in black, and I knew they were going nightwandering.

I ducked out of the way of the window feeling like I was going to puke from nerves. I was desperate to talk to Ti, but I wasn't prepared for her sister. How could I explain what had happened in town with her waving her cigarette around and judging me?

Live true, I reminded myself.

Wimping out of confrontation was what had got me and Ti to this point in the first place.

Downstairs, the living room glowed green from the light of the DVD player. 00:31. This was a second chance, and I wouldn't desert Ti again, no matter what Ophelia said or how poisonous her eyes turned.

'Ti,' I said, opening the door, my voice full of relief.

'Hi,' she said, and she sounded cold and unlike herself.

'I didn't think you'd want to see me.' I spoke quietly, but Ophelia was close enough to hear everything.

'She didn't, but she needs a favour,' she said, chucking her cigarette end on the drive. How could Ti stand to spend so much time with her? She had no manners at all, that was the problem. Getting to know Kiaru and Alisha had made that evident.

'Can I borrow your camera?' Ti said. No please at the end of her request. She seemed tense, not like herself.

'What's going on?'

'Don't pretend you don't know,' Ophelia said, like a psychotic, paranoid person. Her hair was down and she wouldn't leave it alone, pulling it first over one shoulder, and then flicking it to rest across her back. She wiped at the strands that the breeze blew across her forehead, and fixed me with a death stare. '*Everyone* knows.'

I looked to Ti.

'*Chase and Will*,' she whispered. 'Someone told Phe they meet on Saturday nights. She wants evidence.'

'I want to send her to prison,' Ophelia corrected, twisting her hair into a rope. She had begun circling the drive, and it was unnerving. Her attention when it came, was intense, like a spotlight, and I shook my head automatically when she asked if I'd noticed anything at school, relieved that Ti hadn't mentioned what I'd written in my email. I didn't want to be responsible for whatever this was.

'I don't believe you,' Ophelia said. 'You're just too weak to speak up. It makes perfect sense. Getting me out of school. Lying about Ti. She's hiding something. Something big . . .'

Ti looked nervous, and it was clear she wasn't comfortable with this either.

'Is she okay?' I whispered as Ophelia circled to the far end of the drive.

'What do you think?' Ti said, irritated, but with me or Ophelia I couldn't tell.

'Listen Ti, I'm so sorry about today – did you read my emails? I want to make it up to you, I—'

'Rosie, I don't care about that. I just need your camera. *Please*. She's driving me insane.'

She stuck her hand out like she was waiting for change from a shop assistant that had accused her of stealing,

and in this stance, with only the distant street light, she looked so like her sister it was uncanny.

'Ti, you've got to be careful.'

'I'm just helping Phe out. We're not going to get caught.'

I looked towards her sister, who had taken a break from circling, to kick the wall at the end of my drive and light a fresh cigarette.

'Can't you just—'

'You said you wanted to make it up to me.'

So she had read the emails!

'And I do, but this is a stupid idea. Ophelia could go to prison.'

'She won't even be in the garden.'

'Oh.'

'She's gonna wait somewhere else.'

'Please, Ti. I'm so sorry about earlier. It wasn't how it looked.'

'Rosie! I haven't got time for all that now. I need to prove her wrong or she's never going to stop. *Seriously*. Can you just get your camera?'

'Only if I can come with you,' I said, surprising myself. I couldn't bear the way she was cold-shouldering me, though I knew I deserved it.

'What, don't you trust me with it?'

'Course. But I know it better than you. It'll be hard to get a shot in the dark; you'll need a long exposure, so it'll have to be somewhere steady—'

'I'll put it on automatic.'

'It's not as reliable at night. You don't want to mess it up.'

'Can I not just borrow it?'

'Yeah, you *can*. Course you can, but you'll have a better chance if I take the photo. She wants proof, right?'

Ti rolled her eyes, and taking that as permission I crept upstairs to put on my blacks.

Twenty-one

The thrill of roaming empty streets in the dark was absent with Ti ignoring me the way she was. I'd killed the nightwanderers. I'd ruined our only way of escaping the world, and I'd ruined it for both of us. I wanted us to slip into our old ways, for her to make me laugh, and tell me secrets. I wanted her to bring out my brave side, and make me feel like rules didn't matter, but she only walked beside me, refusing to talk. Ophelia strutted ahead.

'Don't pretend you care about my sister,' she said when I asked who had said Chase and Will met like this, and I stopped walking.

'It isn't that I don't *care*. Ti, come on. You must know it isn't that.'

Ti kept on, and I had to run a few steps to catch up with her.

'You don't need to explain anything, Rosie, it doesn't

matter. We've grown apart – it happens – don't worry so much.'

'It *does* matter. And I *want* to explain . . . I feel terrible about how I've neglected you.'

'I'm not an effing dog.'

'No, but—'

'Seriously, Rosie, don't worry about it. We used to have stuff in common and now we don't. You've found new people, it's fine. I'm sure I'll make some friends too soon enough. Anyway, I've got Ophelia. It's *fine*.'

'I just want to explain properly, that's all, I've been feeling so bad—'

'Oh, Rosie, you're so self-involved,' Ti said, and she sounded sad, which surprised me so much that I shut up. But I couldn't walk beside her silent. I didn't know how.

'So much has been happening, Ti, and I've got a lot of things wrong, but you're my best friend.'

Ti snorted.

'You are!'

I'd have to show that I meant what I said. My words had stopped meaning anything to her.

I took photos of Ophelia up ahead in her jeggings and hoody to distract myself from the wretched feeling. She moved like she was famous – the way she held her cigarette, the way she used her hips – I turned to snap Ti against the backdrop of the little bungalows we were passing, and she curled her lip at me.

'You know I hate having my picture taken,' she said, and I turned the camera on myself, stared at the lens gloomily, wondering if a human face was even capable of expressing the misery I felt.

Ophelia was in such a foul mood I wondered why she'd bothered coming with us, and then she left us at the end of Castle Road.

'She's going to check on Will. She's already called the house about eight times. I hope he *is* over at Chase's house. At least she'll snap out of it.'

It was a bit better with only the two of us, and Ti relaxed a little. I told her more about Mum's diagnosis, and how Joey was.

'I miss him,' she admitted.

'He misses you too. You were in one of his pictures the other day. In a spaceship, I think. No, a submarine.'

Ti smiled, and for the billionth time in my life I thanked the universe for my little brother.

Chase's house was almost upon us, and I couldn't believe I was here again. As I held the loose fence panel open for Ti, I saw her teeth gleam in the moonlight. She was smiling wide.

The fence smelled of that varnish men cover it with in the summer, and I realized I'd never seen a woman painting a fence, and swore to paint one when I was older. Wood splintered off as we scraped through into Chase's garden, and it was so easy that I began to relax.

Ti would be careful this time; she had too much to lose. And I would wait with her until the very end. No matter what.

The grass was long and wet underfoot, and I wondered if that meant Chase lived on her own or if she was just too obsessed with rehearsals to maintain the lawn right now. I pushed thoughts of expulsion to the back of my mind. Ti wouldn't go so close to the house again. She wasn't stupid.

A cold wind nipped our ears as we confronted Chase's house from the back of her lawn. It was hard to see how we'd get a clear photo without being seen ourselves. A half moon threw out silvery blue light. If the blinds were lifted, we would be seen.

'We need to knock,' Ti said, heading towards the house. 'Or we'll never get a shot.'

Maybe she *was* stupid.

'Wait!' I hissed. 'You can't knock there. They'll know someone's broken into the garden if you do that.'

Ti stopped in her tracks. 'You're right. Let's throw a stone instead,' she said, heading back to the rockery and crouching down to search for one.

'A *small* one.'

'Duh. *Obviously*. 'Kay, I'll throw, you shoot.'

Finding a rock, she pulled her arm back.

134

'Wait, wait, wait, wait, wait. I need to sort the flash and find a stable place for the camera. It needs a long exposure. And we need to be better hidden . . .'

Why was I even here? Why couldn't I say no to Ti, with her silly ideas, still?

She stuck a branch in the neck of her T-shirt, like a marine, she said, leaves waving in front of her nose, and I felt a rush of love for her.

I looked around for somewhere that offered cover and a flat spot to rest the camera, somewhere that wouldn't obstruct the lens. The feeling in my stomach was closer to fear than excitement, and Mum's pale face flickered into view, but I focused my attention on getting the set-up just right. Ti had to see that she didn't only have her sister: she had me too.

My blood pumping was making things warp. I shook my head to clear it.

'Ready?' she said, and we stared at each other. Me holding out my camera, submerged in a rosemary bush, her clasping a rock with twigs dangling in front of her face.

'Ready,' I said, and then the fence panel creaked, and Ti and me gripped each other in fear. Ophelia hauled herself through the narrow space, and my stomach turned at the sight of her wild expression.

'Dirty little prick!' she shouted, launching her arm back, and before I knew what was happening, there was a loud smash and the front downstairs window shattered.

The floral blind whipped up and Chase appeared. And she wasn't alone.

Twenty-two

Chase and Kes, backlit and horrified, stared into the garden, framed by jagged glass.

Shoving Ophelia out of the way, I rushed from my hiding place and through the loose fence panel, down next door's drive. I wanted to be on tarmac, far away from anyone's garden forever except my own, and Ti was right behind me.

Ophelia was a maniac, now at last Ti could see, so why was she slowing down?

'Wait! Wait! Please, Rosie. I'm scared. She's lost it. Did you see her face? I've had to sleep in her bed every night this week. There's something wrong with her. There's something really wrong with her.'

Ti ducked behind a van and she looked so panicked I couldn't leave.

'This is it,' she said. 'She's going down.' She rubbed her face, and I crouched beside her, and squeezed her to me. 'She won't come back from this.'

'She'll be fine. She's always fine. Just wait.'

Ti was breathing loudly. 'Not this time. It's too much. If Chase calls the police . . . she's already had a warning. God, she couldn't handle prison, Rosie; she's not strong enough.'

'She'll be all right,' I said, and then I realized I didn't have my camera. '*Shit!*'

'I know, where is she?'

'No, I left my camera.'

'You *didn't.*'

'So, we're definitely caught,' I said. 'Your bloody sister.'

'She might have got away.'

'Why do you let her talk you into these things? And why do *I* let *you* talk me into them?'

'I didn't ask you to come. I was just trying to help her. You were the one that—'

'Oh my god,' I said, walking out from where we were hidden. In a house across the road a dog started up yapping and the hairs on the back of my neck stood on end, because it was really dawning on me. 'You're *never* going to learn, are you?'

'She's my sister, Rosie. What am I supposed to do?' Ti stepped from foot to foot, peering into the distance towards Chase's house.

'You're not helping her, you know. You think you are, but you're not.'

She turned to me like she was about to get angry, but

a car was coming, and so she ducked back behind the van instead. I joined her, and we crouched as a black BMW crawled by.

'I'm going back.'

'Don't be an idiot, Ti. Leave her. If she's caught, it's her own dumb fault, and there's nothing you can do. Maybe she needs to be sent down, before she gets any worse.'

But Ti was already heading back towards the house.

'What are you going to do to help? Offer yourself up as well? Swap places with her? Jesus!'

'I just need to make sure she's all right.'

'What do you think you're going to achieve?'

I grabbed at her hands, but she wouldn't stop. 'I'm going home, Ti, and you should go too. You're stupid if you think you're helping.'

'You're stupid if you think I have a choice. She's my *sister*, Rosie. My *twin* sister. Imagine if it was Joey.'

'Joey's a good person.'

'Piss off, Rosie, Joey's eight years old. He hasn't even got pubes. Imagine he was fifteen, the same age as you, same height. That you'd known him since before you were born. Oh, what's the point? Go home. You can't understand. No one can.'

She was right. I couldn't understand and I was tired of trying.

'I don't need you pretending to be my friend because you feel guilty.'

139

'What? As if . . . Come on, Ti . . .'

'I mean it, Rosie. You don't need to feel bad for me any more.'

Ti kept walking, back in the direction she should have been running from, and it was so frustrating that I had to pull at the roots of my hair just to release some of the pressure.

'Fine. You're on your own,' I called after her. 'Just you and your crazy sister. See where it gets you. Maybe you can share a cell in prison.'

Ti stuck her finger up, without looking back.

She didn't care what I thought or said. She was on automatic, chasing after her sister like always, no matter how much trouble it meant.

Twenty-three

'Not you, Rosie,' Chase said, as I filed out the class with Alisha and Kiaru. It was the end of Drama the following Monday, and I'd been having palpitations since Saturday night. I hadn't heard from Ti and I was determined not to care. I couldn't even think of Ophelia without getting seriously angry. Kiaru and Alisha looked scared for me, and my throat constricted. Here it came.

Charlie smirked as she left the classroom, lagging behind to see if she could glean a bit of gossip.

'Close the door, please, Charlie,' Chase said firmly. Her red hair was twisted into pin curls, and she looked stylish as ever, in a green polka dot tea dress. She was neatening a pile of worksheets, a delay tactic, and I prayed the moment of calm would last forever.

'Yes, Ms,' Charlie sang as she shut the door. I heard her musical laughter ring out in the hall.

Chase's eyes met mine. Blue and precise. There was no escaping. She had never paid me such attention before, and I shivered.

'This weekend,' she said. 'What happened?'

I swallowed instead of speaking.

'You were in my garden,' she continued, but something about the way she said it made me think she wasn't certain.

'Sorry?' I said, imagining I was Alisha or Ava, very confident and together, and perfectly polite.

'Stop it,' she snapped. 'You're still close with Titania, and for some reason I can't guess – believe me I've spent the weekend trying – you were in my garden on Saturday night.'

I made my face blank.

'Trespassing is a serious issue, Rosie, I'm not sure if you realize. Titania was very nearly arrested. *Again.*'

'What happened?' I said, and Ms Chase narrowed her eyes, refusing to indulge what she clearly saw as my pretence of innocence. I almost owned up, just to find out what had happened to Ti. Had she gone back and knocked on Chase's door? I hadn't contacted Ti. Maybe I never would again. Maybe she was right, and we really had grown apart.

'It's a criminal offence, trespassing – do you even realize that? Listen to me, Rosie. I'm trying to help you.'

She let a big breath out, and looked at me in that searching way adults try when they aren't sure whether you can understand or not. When they aren't sure what approach to try next.

'I don't know what's going on with the pair of you, but it isn't going to end well, and you really need to get yourself out of it. Titania wasn't a good student, and neither was her sister, and I know she's angry, but she, *they*, need to let this, this *thing* – whatever it is – go.

'I don't know if it's a game or a dare or what, but I can't stand any more of it, and they're going to get into grave trouble if they carry on. I'm *this close* to getting an injunction against her. Ophelia's sneaky, I can't pin it on her, but Ti got caught again. I could pin her, easy. Do you want to visit Titania in a juvenile-delinquency centre? Because if you don't, I recommend you say something *soon*.

'I mean it, Rosie. If you have any influence over Titania at all, *at all*, you've got to try to make her see sense. This "beef" – whatever it is – *has* to stop. Do you understand?'

Chase seemed shaken and I wondered if she was putting it on, because how scary was it, really? Having your window smashed by teenage girls?

'Maybe it's the naughty kids at The Bridge, having a bad influence on her,' I said quietly, and Chase's eyes flashed on to mine.

'Oh no,' she said, and she seemed to be struggling to stay professional. 'I'm not having that. People need to take responsibility. That's what they don't teach any more. If those girls don't take responsibility for their choices, *they'll* pay for it. Nobody else.

'You're not a bad kid, just easily led. There's no shame in it; Titania's a charismatic girl – but I'm telling you, Rosie – stick with your new friends, focus on your work. Because those girls are going to get nothing but what they've asked for.'

After an intense look that I thought would never end, she nudged her head towards the door, and it took every bit of power I had not to sprint out of it.

The corridor was seething, and at first I thought it was the usual mixture of theatre kids and hangers-on, coming to ask Chase a question or deliver a prop, but they were crowding round something, and pushing my way to the front I saw what it was. An A4 sheet of paper in the middle of the Drama noticeboard.

The photograph.

It was the first time I'd seen it, and I couldn't help noticing the quality of the image. My instinct must have made me press the shutter release, in spite of the shock.

Chase and Kes, looking guilty, amidst shattering glass.

'Did you take that?' Kiaru whispered, at the edge of the crowd.

Alisha gripped my arm. 'Does she know you were there?'

Kids gasped and hooted, the noise getting louder until it was like sports day, and then Chase's door opened.

'What's going on out here? Knock on my door if you want to see me, otherwise, out of the Drama block!'

Lost in the mass of other kids leaving, we turned to watch as Chase examined the poster. There was the sound of paper ripping as she pulled it down.

Twenty-four

At the start of last lesson a prefect arrived to tell the teacher I was required in Kes's office. Seeing we were all too excited about finishing school at the end of the week to concentrate on land reforms, Mr Hedges had admitted defeat and let us play Monopoly, and I moved my counter six places before collecting my stuff, thinking of the way Ti always finished what she was doing before she exited a classroom. 'It gives the illusion of being in control,' she had once said.

It was unusual to be the centre of everyone's attention, but I could see how you might get used to it. Crave it even.

Kiaru watched from the adjacent table, and I wondered if he was impressed or disappointed.

It was almost a relief walking there. The doors of the teachers' offices passed by me like pieces of set from a film. So much had happened in the last couple of weeks that I half wanted to be punished. It would be nice to stop hiding things and avoiding people and sneaking around.

Katy Johnson, the prefect escorting me, knocked on the door to Kes's office, then opened it for me to enter.

Inside, Chase sat with her legs crossed, hands clasped in her lap, lips pressed together. Kes sat behind his desk, upon which was the poster.

My adrenalin level spiked, my cheeks hot, but I met their eyes. Ti had said she'd felt they were united against her when she was brought in, and I did too. What exactly was the deal between them? Was it Kes's shadow we'd seen that first time at Chase's? And did that mean he knew Chase was lying about Ti? The stuffed mole burrowed up to the light, and I held my breath, wishing for an underground lair of my own to creep into.

Chase glanced at Kes, who pursed his lips.

'Titania De Furia has implicated you,' he said, and there was no chance to deny it, because there on the desk was the self-portrait I'd taken of me with a bleak expression.

'The time matches the break-in,' Chase said, and I noticed the blurry orange figures in the bottom right corner. I hated the date feature, and never used it, but Dad had taken my camera on a protest recently, and he loved the date stamp because he hoped to capture the police doing something incriminating. In my rush to leave with Ti I hadn't noticed it was still on. Not that I'd expected it to be used against me.

'We don't know or want to know the motives behind your scheming. We simply don't have time for this kind of behaviour here. You've proven yourself a capable student, but weak-willed and sly, and your presence is not appreciated at this time. Do you understand, Miss Bloom?'

Chase blinked in my direction. 'Perhaps you've been placing your loyalty in the wrong areas,' she said, and there was a smug look in her blue eyes, because she'd known I was lying, and now I was caught.

'Miss Bloom?' Kes said, and I realized he was waiting for an answer.

'I understand,' I said, though I didn't completely.

Chase rose at the same time as Kes, and we all walked out of the cluttered office into the starker space of the corridors together. A first year carrying a box of folders stared at me and my shocked red face like I was a one-armed foetus emerging from a bottle of formaldehyde.

'Time for a big think, eh, Rosie?' Chase said, holding her hand out so I had to shake it, and then she turned towards her beloved Drama block, vintage heels clicking, off to yet another *Grease* dress rehearsal.

Kes walked me very slowly to the main doors by reception. My own personal funeral march.

'Ms Chase is right. Time for a very big think indeed.

Consider the type of person you want to be, Rosie, and what you want to make of yourself. Think about how you've been spending your time lately, how you would like to spend it in future. The kind of people you want to put your faith in. This matter is far from closed.'

He held his hand out for me to shake, and then his huge dry palm was in mine, and the door was shutting, and it was me on the wrong side of it this time, with all my friends inside.

Twenty-five

Dawdling home in a daze, I tried out explanations, but none were acceptable, and pushing the door handle I felt I was walking into a stranger's house.

Dad was chopping without looking, the way he always did, the way he'd learned back when he was a chef, before I was born. He swiped the ingredients into a pan, wiping his knife on the tea towel he had tucked in his waistband. I thought maybe he hadn't heard me come in, that I could creep to my bedroom, like the worm that I was, but then he spoke.

'Sit down.'

Dad could make delicious dinners with his eyes closed, slicing and singing and messing around, but right now the kitchen was silent except for his knife.

De-de-de-de-de-de-de-de-de-de-de-de-de-de.

My brain scanned for justifications as I sat, but there

were none. And then he turned and the look he gave me made the lump in my throat double.

'You *stupid*, *horrible* little girl,' he said, and I almost fell off my chair. 'We can't cope with you getting into trouble, can you not understand that? I'm run off my feet as it is – I can't afford to be dragged out of work like this for something so . . . I thought you of all people knew. I've been on the phone to your Drama teacher this afternoon. She called me at work, thank god. Can you imagine if she'd called home? Spoken to your mum? With this talk of suspension. What's going on, Rosie? Creeping around at night, a campaign against your teachers – what were you thinking?'

I had no answer, but I had to say something.

'I didn't put the posters up,' I said. 'I don't know who did that, it must have been—'

'But you did break into your teacher's garden? In the middle of the night. And smash the window?'

'No! That wasn't me, that was Ophelia, she—'

'But you did take the photograph, didn't you? Admit that at least. You can't wriggle out of that one, thanks to your *good friend Titania*. And you were there through all of it, which makes you guilty by association. How could you be so stupid? I thought you were a clever girl. It's embarrassing, Rosie. I'm *embarrassed*.' He pleaded instead of shouting, and that made it worse somehow.

'You won't be using that camera again, I'll tell you

that for free. Where is it? Bring it here. *This* is *not* what I gave it to you for.'

'I don't know where it is,' I admitted miserably.

'Careless as well! You're really pulling out all the stops, eh? Your teacher used the word "stalking", Rosie. She mentioned the police. Do you realize how serious that is? You're nearly sixteen, for Christ's sake, use your bloody brain. Creeping around gardens in the middle of the night? A vendetta against your teacher? It makes you sound *unhinged*.'

The onions and peppers were burning in the pan, and I couldn't believe it because Dad was like a machine in the kitchen. It was his happy place, where he did everything absolutely right. Mum always put the oil on before she'd even chopped the vegetables, getting it so hot it burned everything before she'd begun, and Dad couldn't understand – he called her untrainable – and now here he was, ruining the vegetables because I was such a disappointment he couldn't cook straight.

I lay my head on my arms, dying to get away for one second, and then Dad started shrieking, except it wasn't Dad it was the fire alarm, and we both jumped up with tea towels to waft underneath the sensor before the racket disturbed Mum.

'I don't need this, Rosie,' Dad said, slightly out of breath, the electronic shriek finally silenced, and his voice cracked. 'I don't *need* it.'

'I was trying to help Ti,' I said quietly. 'That's why I went. I haven't been a good friend to her, and she needed my camera and then—'

'Jesus Christ on a stick! I don't want to hear you defending her any more, Rosie. She's the one that got you into this mess. A good friend wouldn't ask you to do something that would get you into trouble, can you not see? A *good friend* wouldn't ask you to do something that put you in danger. When are you going to learn? I cannot for the life of me understand —'

I tried to say she hadn't asked me, she'd just wanted my camera, but he wasn't listening. He spun back to the hob to chuck a tin of tomatoes into the seething pot.

'Ms Chase believes that Ti and her sister have a hold on you, that you're under their influence—'

'What? That's ridiculous, as if—'

'— *so, if you're very lucky*, you might get another chance. She said you're doing better in lessons, that your new friends take school seriously, but from what she said you're also a liar and a sneak, and they aren't sure what to make of you.'

'*Dad, please, listen*, it's not like you think . . .'

'I'm sorry, Rosie, I don't believe a word that comes out your mouth. No more Titania, that's the first thing. No phone calls. No emails. No meeting in secret. No planning or plotting or scheming, nothing like that. You aren't good for each other. You know, we thought we'd been

153

lucky with you – so helpful and gentle and kind – we thought *this is too good to be true*. And now . . . ? I don't know. I can't get my head round it. You're not who I thought you were, Rosie. You're not. And it bloody *hurts*.'

'*Dad.*' My voice was unrecognizable, and I wanted so much to make him listen, but to what? I had no excuse. Everything he was saying about me was true.

'Just thank your lucky stars they called me at work, because I can't risk your mum falling again, not now when we're just getting close—'

'See! *This* is what I mean!' A feeling of injustice surged through me, and I stood up. '*This* is why I sneak around, because Mum's always just about to get better, if only *I* don't mess everything up! Well, it's impossible, and it isn't fair. I'm not even sixteen! I'm a *child*! Why can't I just have a normal mum? That gets up and helps around the house and has conversations and *does* things? It's like she's *dead*. She's not a real person! She might as well be dead! Least then I could have a life!'

I stood by the table, breathing hard. I could hear ringing in my ears. It *was* like Mum had died. I hadn't realized I thought that until I shouted it out loud, and now I couldn't take it back.

Dad's hand still clutched a sauce-coated spatula, and he stared back, nostrils flaring, angry enough that it crossed my mind he could hit me. I thought of Ophelia, and how Ti had told me that Fab had slapped her face that time he

154

caught her stealing, and I wondered what I would do if Dad did that now. I'd probably just let him. I deserved it.

'I'm sorry. Dad? I'm *sorry*. I didn't mean that. I didn't want to upset you, I—'

'Don't! I mean it. You didn't want to upset me? Well, you have. You've bloody cut me to the quick. I thought you were better than this. I thought you had compassion, integrity, but I'm starting to think that it's all been lies. Who *exactly* is this standing in front of me? Because it's not my Rose.'

He stirred overzealously, splashing tomatoes on the tiles above the hob, and I couldn't hold down the hatches any more.

'*Daddy*.' Tears with snot for good luck, and my voice like a baby's.

'At least with Titania she's honest about who she is. At least with her what you see is what you get.'

The sauce was burning again on the bottom of the pan, and I wanted to tell him to turn the heat down, but I didn't dare. It felt like I'd lost the right to tell him to do anything ever again, and I left the kitchen instead, feeling the whole mess I'd got myself into, and the mess our family was in, and what a bad friend I'd been to Ti, and how none of it had helped anyone.

Life couldn't get any worse, I thought, and then I saw Mum, crouched on the bottom stair, with her head against the wall, eyes screwed shut like a little kid.

Twenty-six

'*Dad*,' I called, and something in my voice made him come to me without question.

'*Shit*,' he muttered. 'Lucy.'

She looked at us with such pain, and I wondered why she wasn't saying anything, then realized that she couldn't. Her mouth moved, but no sound came out, and her lips had lost all their pinkness; they looked floury and dry like they needed some balm. I prayed that she hadn't been there for long. Her usually glossy chestnut hair hung limp over her shoulders.

'Go to your room, Rosie,' Dad said, and I was so ashamed that I ran straight past her, without speaking, up the stairs and to my bed where I pulled the duvet over my head. How long had she been there? How much had she heard?

Footsteps on the stairs, and Dad's low voice soothing. Maybe he could make everything okay. The things I'd said played in my mind, and it was like a hot needle piercing my brain.

'I heard the fire alarm!' Mum's voice lifted abruptly. 'What did you expect? Let *go* of my arm; I'm not an invalid!'

I closed my eyes.

'Don't shout, Lucy, please,' Dad said in his infuriatingly low voice.

'I'll shout if I bloody want! This is *my* house! *My* family! Stop suppressing everybody, Alistair. Stop putting everybody on eggshells. Rosie! *Rosie!* I know you can hear this! Come out here!'

They were on the landing outside my room now, and I was filled with dread as I dragged myself out of bed. Mum held on to the banister, and Dad fixed me with a dark expression.

'Don't listen to your dad when he tells you not to worry me. Do you hear? I'm still your mother and I *demand* to worry! It's my human right. Do you understand me?'

Joey burst out of his room in his school uniform, looking scared. Dad must have collected him on his way back from the uni. 'What's happening?'

'God, I'm so *lonely*!' Mum wailed. 'You all get me grapes and cards and visit, and I know what you're trying to do, and it's sweet, but it makes me so *lonely*. It makes me feel like the only thing I am is an ill person.

Like there's nothing else left, and all I really want is my bloody family to bloody well talk to me!'

Letting out a shout of frustration, she put her face in her hands, and Dad took her elbow, because it was obvious that this walk downstairs had taken it out of her.

'Come on, Luce,' Dad said. 'This isn't helping anyone. Let's get you back to bed, and then we can talk. Rosie will be honest with you, lay it all out, won't you, Rosie?'

I nodded, but did he really want me to be honest or just say what Mum wanted to hear, and how was I supposed to know the difference? And all the while, Mum being too tired to stand spoke more powerfully than anything else, because the truth – whether any of us liked it or not – was that it didn't matter what she wanted or what I wanted or what Dad wanted, because in the end her bloody illness got to decide.

Twenty-seven

The next morning, I felt very calm and grown up. Everything was different and I was alone. Nobody understood me, and that was fine. Dad had confiscated my laptop and phone, and told me that for the rest of the week Mum was my responsibility. I wasn't allowed to go back to Fairfields until after the holidays, which was okay by me seeing as everyone must think me a psycho stalker now too. I would make Mum's lunches and keep the house clean, and focus on my schoolwork, Dad said. My social life was on hold until I could be trusted.

'We'll make you responsible yet,' he said, and our eyes rested very coolly on each other.

So, he was disappointed. Well, I was disappointed too. All the times I'd collected Joey and made the dinner and done the laundry and taken messages in my best phone voice counted for nothing. Now I was just like everyone else who put pressure on him and didn't understand, just another problem.

I put a wash on, and took up Mum's lunch tray, and read her another chapter of *What Katy Did*, while she did an elaborate French plait in my hair. We hadn't talked about what I'd said, but I heard my words when I was trying to fall asleep. *She might as well be dead.* What kind of person said things like that? No wonder I wasn't allowed outdoors.

'It's getting so long,' Mum said, securing the end of the plait with a bobble. 'You'll have to ask your dad to take you to Ryan's for a trim.'

'Mmm,' I said, though I wouldn't be asking Dad for anything.

Drinking tea later, in the kitchen, I did my Maths pages, and it was refreshing not to have my phone or computer, to know that I couldn't communicate with anyone even if I wanted to.

Arguing with Dad I'd sounded exactly like Ti defending Ophelia. And he was right – a good friend wouldn't ask me to do something dangerous. But Ti hadn't asked.

He preferred to think Ti had all the power, that I was too weak to decide for myself, but what was the truth? I couldn't work it out. There was no way Ti would have 'implicated' me; Chase must have found my camera where I dropped it, that was all.

160

What did Alisha and Kiaru think about me now? What was going around school? It was peculiar, feeling so detached, but it was a relief too. Emotions made me do ridiculous stuff. I couldn't trust them.

Dad seemed apologetic when he returned from work. He'd never shouted at me like that before, or called me a *horrible little girl*, and maybe he felt bad about it (like I had yesterday, when I'd still had feelings).

He thanked me for making the house look nice, and asked how Mum was, and I answered in a robotic way. He looked over my work, and offered to slice up an apple for me, but I didn't want an apple. I didn't want anything.

After dinner – brown rice and leftover chilli that I couldn't eat – I went to my room and stared at the ceiling. For the first time in weeks, I didn't worry about a thing.

At six o'clock the phone rang, and my heart began racing. Maybe it was Ti calling to make friends, to say she'd felt sick since Saturday night as well. But what would Dad say to her? I ran to the landing to listen, surprised when, after a few seconds he shouted for me.

'I thought you said no phone.'

He moved his head slightly, a kind of shrug. 'It's

Alisha,' he said, and I was annoyed on Ti's behalf. Five years she'd been coming round here. He'd met Alisha once, and already she was in the inner sanctum.

'Hello?'

'Rosie! What the hell? How are you? What's going on?'

I stared blankly at Dad until he walked away. 'Nothing, I'm fine. How are you? How's school?'

'You sound different. Are you okay? What happened? Everyone's saying Chase got an injunction against you, that Ti's been arrested. Is it true you're not coming back?'

'I'm coming back. I think.'

'Oh. Well. Phew! Are you all right? You don't sound all right.'

'I'm all right,' I said, only I couldn't get the words out. I remembered Ti, crying at the top of the slide at the Beacon, and how I'd sworn to do whatever it took to help her.

'Rosie? Tell me what happened,' Alisha said, but I couldn't stop crying for long enough.

'Talk later,' I managed in a broken jumble, and then I put my head in my hands.

Joey tiptoed out of his room, and I tried to get myself together, but all control had gone.

'What is *happening* around here?' he said as I stood up,

162

hiding my face so as not to alarm him. 'Why won't anyone talk to me?'

I was no longer his Rose, that's what Dad had said. And he was right; I felt it.

So who was I?

Twenty-eight

The next evening, there was a knock on the door after dinner, and a few minutes later Dad came up to my room with a purple folder.

'That was your friends at the door,' he said, meaning my *authorized* friends. 'They took some notes for you. They say hello. They hope you're all right.'

I took the folder wordlessly, and Dad stood by my bed for a minute, fiddling with a thread dangling from the sleeve of his tweed jacket, before leaving.

The folder contained school-related notes from English and Science in Alisha and Kiaru's writing, and I scanned them, disappointed, until I reached the final page. Following the conclusion subheading was a paragraph headed *Party*.

We're working on your dad, Alisha had written. *See you after the play on Friday.*

Ava's party, I'd forgotten. Alisha wrote that the

rumour about Chase and Will was all over school, and that people were saying Chase was having an affair with him behind Kes's back. Kes had delivered a whole-school assembly about the importance of respecting teachers' rights to private lives, which Chase was mysteriously absent from, and Will had avoided everyone's eyes the whole time.

You have to come out on Friday, Alisha had written in her swirly handwriting. *Kiaru wants you to be there*, then she'd drawn a heart that sent my blood pressure soaring.

The rest of the week passed in a similar pattern: I made Mum's trays, and kept her company, telling her just enough about how I was to make her feel less lonely. Or so I hoped. Joey badgered me to play *Guitar Hero* with him, and asked why I wasn't talking to Dad, and I fobbed him off by telling him I was on my period, which he didn't understand at all, and so shut up.

After dinner, the doorbell would ring as Alisha and/ or Kiaru brought a new batch of schoolwork. Dad wouldn't let me speak to them myself or pass anything back, but I listened on the stairs as he talked to them, and they stayed for longer each visit.

We're working on your dad, Alisha had written, and I hated how confident she was. I didn't want my dad to be swayed by charm and scheming. He was always saying how he valued authenticity over everything else, but when it came to it he was as easily fooled as anyone.

Twenty-nine

When Dad called me at sixish the next night I headed downstairs with my hair messy enough that he wouldn't think I was presuming anything.

Kiaru stood at the door in his tight jeans and huge parka, alone, and my disappointment at Dad's inconsistency exploded into joy. The weather had turned wintery, although it was March, and Kiaru's parka finally made sense. I could feel the first smile of the week attempting to bust my face open, but I wouldn't let Dad see it.

'Kiaru has said he'll walk you to this party of Ava's, and get you home for nine, so how about I handle dinner tonight?'

'Okay,' I said flatly.

'Because I *do* want you to have friends, Rosie, and I want you to see that.'

I shrugged, forcing myself to stay quiet. He wanted

me to have friends; he just didn't believe I was intelligent enough to choose them for myself.

'So, *nine o'clock,*' he said firmly, like every dad from every teen movie ever, and for a horrible second I thought Kiaru was going to say, 'Yes, sir,' but thankfully he just nodded and turned his attention to me.

'It's pretty cold out,' he said. 'You might need more layers.'

I ran upstairs and grabbed my duffle coat and Mum's cream woolly hat, and walking back to the kitchen I could hear him talking to Dad about the weather as though it were an actual subject, and I felt depressed that adults were so easy to manipulate.

'Right you are,' I said to break up their chat about when exactly the storm was going to hit, and how likely we were to get caught in it on our way home, and Dad looked weirdly timid as he handed me his oversized golf umbrella. I pulled a face, because it was ridiculous, but Kiaru took it seamlessly, as though Dad had been passing it to him all along. He made everything smooth like hazelnut butter, and it was impressive to witness, but there was something cold about it too, and I thought of Ti, fidgeting and interrupting and whispering and nudging, and I missed her.

'Right you are,' Kiaru said, taking my cue. With the umbrella tucked under his arm like one of the Rat Pack, he followed me over the threshold of my house, and allowing my smile free reign finally, I ran into the night, exhilarated by possibility.

The sun hadn't set yet, and it was still light, though the sky was crowded with blueish-charcoal cloud. Walking together along Erissey Terrace we stared out at a fishing boat heading into the harbour, a swarm of herring gulls trailing behind it like a bad thought.

'Thanks for the notes,' I said.

'You're welcome. We didn't want you to get behind. You've only just caught up.'

Moored boats bobbed gently on the uneasy water, and my stomach rocked with them as we walked in silence. I was happy to be out here with him, but I was worried about Ti too – it had been almost a whole week now without her sneaking me a phone call, and every time I thought about our argument I got a lump in my throat.

'So what happened?' Kiaru asked, after a couple of minutes of silence, and I started to explain about Chase's garden round two, and how it related to the milkshake shop, that somehow Ti had got caught, though it was Ophelia that had smashed the window. I told him how Mum and Dad thought Ti was bad for me, and how I thought they were wrong but I was worried too, because what if I was delusional the way Ti was about Ophelia? I never wanted to be blind like that.

Kiaru listened, asking occasional questions, and soon we had walked through town and were on Castle Road, cutting on to the coast path, then heading down the steep cliff to Durgan. This wasn't where Ava's party was, but I didn't feel like a party.

We found a low flat rock to sit and watch the waves coming in, and I wished I hadn't lost my camera because it would be so great to photograph Kiaru against the unsettled sea. I found a thread of seaweed, and tried to pop the bubbles at its ends.

'Bladderwrack,' I said.

'Huh?'

'This is called bladderwrack. Ti taught me that. She's in love with the sea.'

Kiaru stared out at it, surging and gigantic just ahead of us. 'Aren't we all?'

'She loves it so much, she wrote *mermaid* as her number one aspiration on her work experience form.'

Kiaru smiled. 'I wrote international man of mystery on mine.'

'Did you?'

'No, of course not. I wrote potter.'

'Did you!?'

'No! Why can't you tell when I'm joking?'

'Because you never change the tone of your voice! So what did you write? Seriously.'

'I wrote GP, because my dad has had my work

placement lined up at his practice since I was a toddler. Deal is that I have to at least try it before he'll allow me to choose some "airy fairy" course at university.'

'Wow.'

'What did you write?'

'I wrote photographer, but Mr Starkey said we didn't have any of those on the work experience books, so I wrote photography teacher instead.'

'Aim for the stars and you just might hit the moon.'

'That's what Ti said!'

'Ti sounds *hilarious*.'

'She is. She's the funniest person I know. She's an idiot as well though. She makes the stupidest decisions.'

I threw a small rock at the no swimming sign a few metres away, missed, and tried again. The beach here shelved dramatically, so it was hard to climb out if the water was rough or you weren't a strong swimmer. Every year somebody died. Usually a tourist that didn't know any better.

'I can sort of see why my parents don't want us to be friends to be honest.'

Kiaru aimed, and missed, and I looked for the perfect-sized rock.

'They don't get to decide, though, do they? It's up to you. You just have to show them that it's a real friendship, that you won't let them get in the way.'

'I don't think she wants to be friends any more. She says we've grown apart.'

'She's hurt. People are delicate, you know.'

'That doesn't make me feel better,' I said, taking aim.

'Why not? It should – oh! You got it! Nice one! – it means she cares about you, which means she'll want to make up. And you obviously care about her. Just tell your dad you've listened to what he said, and you've thought it through carefully, and he's wrong. Tell him it's not up to him to choose who your friends are . . .'

The sheer sense in that made me wonder why I hadn't managed to say it in the first place, and we sat quietly for a minute listening to the water.

'I have an admission to make,' he said after a while.

'Uh-huh.'

'This isn't Ava's fancy dress party.'

'I wondered where all the people were . . .'

'I just wanted to sit somewhere with you for a bit first.'

With you.

'I actually lied to your dad.'

'But you were so convincing!'

'I know, I feel grotty. Never tell him. Do you still want to hang out with me? I mean, do you feel safe?'

'I feel a bit frightened. Who even are you?' I said, and our voices bubbled with all the extra stuff we weren't saying, and there was this huge swell of excitement in me, bigger than all the storm clouds combined, because perfect, virtuous Kiaru had lied to my dad so he could sit somewhere *with me*.

171

'You know, when Alisha first picked you out, I wasn't sure.'

'Thank you.'

'You're like the most tightly closed book on the shelf.'

'*You're* the most tightly closed book on the shelf! You're like a book that has superglued its pages together, and then vacuum-packed itself, and then fed itself through a mangle.'

He laughed. Again! I could make him laugh!

'I could see you were pretty, but I didn't expect you to have such . . . hidden depths.'

I was hardly listening to the end of his sentence because I was so delighted by the start. I already suspected I was interesting, if people got to know me – I didn't care about that so much – what I wanted was for someone to think I was pretty. Call me shallow, if you like.

'You shouldn't write people off so easily,' I said, and I was joking, but he answered seriously.

'I really shouldn't,' he said, and standing he held his hands out. As he pulled me up we were close together, and I hoped he'd try to kiss me, but he only jumped from the rock, and I blushed though no one was looking.

'Wonder if we can get on to the roof,' I shouted over the music. It was some terrible picked-off-TV girl singer

172

convinced she was bleeding love, and my ears hurt. Ava had settled on a rainbow theme in the end, and the crowd was multi-coloured, huddled in corners, and downing drinks or smoking. What I really wanted was to be outside with Kiaru again. It was something I hadn't really felt before, like all these other people were just in the way.

Palm Beach Hotel had been a decadent palace years ago, but was now a wreck. Disco lights flash-bombed the lavish peeling wallpaper, and a grand staircase spiralling upwards had become a kind of elaborate bench, with kids on every step, kissing and laughing and drinking from cans and glass bottles.

We'd found a makeshift bar in a manky-looking ex-swimming pool. A strobe lit up the old waterline as well as the scum in the corners, and some kid I didn't know handed us small bottles of beer.

Outside, palm trees flapped their leaves in the wind and gulls surfed the air currents above them. You could just hear the ocean over the sounds of the party, though you couldn't see it because of a thick hedge around the gardens. Jesse Burzyinski and Tommy O'Shea were pressed against a monkey puzzle tree, and another couple were lying together on the ground though it wasn't completely dark yet. I pulled my coat round me, glad of Mum's hat, and looked for the fire stairs.

Kiaru held his hand out for me to go first.

'Right. If the stairs collapse, the lady takes the spinal injury,' I said.

'Girls just wanna have fun times in the hospital,' he said, and we trudged upwards, passing four different floors of balconies, each littered with the inevitable smokers and snoggers. What Kiaru had said made sense. I would get in touch with Ti first thing tomorrow, no matter what Dad said. I would make him listen and he would understand. The wind blew in off the sea, and it all seemed so simple.

We didn't stop until we got to the roof, and I moved fast, imagining Kiaru was impressed by my agility and love of heights. I climbed faster, feeling like a mountain goat, the sexy kind that gets the guy.

The wind made us duck our heads, but the roof was perfect: flat and surrounded by a wall that you could sit on, swinging your legs if you had the stomach for it, which I did. I convinced Kiaru to join me, and we sat, refreshing our feet in imaginary water.

Counting the tankers on the horizon – there were always more than you first thought – I sipped my horrible beer. How many teen deaths must result from this precise recipe: alcohol, heights, bravado.

I felt Kiaru looking at me, and turning to him it shocked me for a second how smooth his skin was, and how comfortable we'd become together.

Now it was his turn to stare at the horizon.

In the distance the shadowy sky blurred where it rained over the sea. The wind built and music thumped a rhythm below us, and Kiaru didn't seem at all concerned about getting wet. Like Ti that first day in the playground: all the best people didn't mind a bit of rain.

He was looking at me again, there was no mistake. My hair blew on to my face, and he put it behind my ear, sending shivers through every bit of me, and I held my breath, aware of how close he was, and how high up we were. Vertigo, the very best kind, out of nowhere.

'*Rosie Bloom,*' he said, as though my name were italicised in his head, and his breath was beery, but not in a bad way, and I was about to say how much I liked him, when I realized that there were other ways to communicate.

His eyes closed as I leaned into him, and the thought of us tumbling from the fifth floor only improved the feeling as we kissed. His thumb stroked the back of my neck, the nerves jangling up and down my spine, and he put his arm round me and pulled me closer, so warm, and somewhere in the distance the rain started. Birds hid and waves crashed, and whatever happened out there, in that black streak on the horizon, I wouldn't be the one who suggested home.

Thirty

We couldn't tell the alarm was coming from school until we were so close it was deafening.

We ran up the drive to investigate, remembering it was show night, as teachers, parents and kids streamed into the car park, looking frightened. There was a burnt smell in the air, but it could have been a bonfire, people lit their garden waste all the time. Somebody had set the alarm off for a prank, that was our assumption. Until Chase sprinted out the gym with a frantic expression. In a fifties-style tea dress and high heels, she pushed through the dazed audience, and made for the Drama block.

T-Birds and Pink Ladies from the cast looked around for their families while the screech of the alarm cut through everything, hurting my ears and stressing everyone out. I thought of Dad, flapping his tea towel – I was due home; we had been on our way – but I couldn't leave without knowing what was happening.

The spring air was icy, and no one was wearing enough clothes, except for me and Kiaru. I pulled Mum's hat down further over my ears, grateful to him for suggesting it. Mums and dads and grandparents pulled spring coats round themselves, dipping heads into collars.

Kes had walked to the centre of the playground and was shouting orders, but we couldn't hear him over the alarm and the calls of panicked parents and the wind. Beside him, Mr Miles waved his arms for people to make their way towards him, but nobody moved in his direction.

Petals from the crab-apple trees spun in the air all around us, and scanning the crowd for Alisha, Kiaru and I huddled together for warmth. A petal landed on the furry hood of his parka, and I imagined we were the centrepiece in a Fairfields snow dome as the pink fragments churned round us. Wind roared in my ears and pushed at my back, then my front, tunnelling under my coat and through my layers.

Two fire engines arrived, blasting their sirens. They drove straight from the car park into the playing fields, and we followed the flashing blue lights, in spite of Mr Miles's orders not to. Word rippled through the crowd: this was no false alarm.

Charlie came up to us frothing with news, still in her Pink Ladies jacket. 'It's the Drama block,' she said, round-eyed. 'Chase is totally hysterical. Crying and everything. Don't worry though, Kiaru, Alisha's over there.'

'Thank god,' Kiaru said, and we ran over to hug her. At the same moment the whole crowd began running – parents, toddlers, grandparents. We all ran towards the fire. More sirens could be heard in the distance, and a police car drove through the crowd, then an ambulance. Kiaru's face flashed blue and he grabbed for my hand.

'Can you smell smoke?' we asked each other, unsure if we were imagining it, but it was becoming undeniable: a thick poisonous cloud wafted over us, scorching our noses and throats.

Police pushed us back, ordering us to leave so they could do their job, but nobody listened. We couldn't. There were too many of us needing to know what was going on. Parents clustered in small groups with their kids and their kids' friends, watching in disbelief as tall men with shaved heads and dirty, yellow overalls pulled out rolls of hose, the textbook choreography of fire.

Water began trickling from the hose, then spraying, then a full gust shot into the Drama block, and the smoke began to blacken and thicken. Head prefects Katy Johnson and Ethan Crisp joined the police and firemen in shouting at everyone to stay back. Red and white safety tape appeared, and still the crowd pushed forward, determined to get a proper view of the school as it burned. We gasped together, as though at a fireworks display.

178

It was incomputable.

Flames raged out of the top of what had been the Drama block, as a stream of water arced into the building. Droplets sprayed onto our faces and the smoke glowed orange against the dark sky, the wind whipping sparks and ash to land in people's hair and on their shoulders.

'The rain,' I said, and Kiaru nodded. It was coming. We'd seen it.

Kes must have run with the rest of us, because he now stood at the front of the opposite side of the crowd, watching with his hands over his mouth as the windows began to explode. Inside the building, something collapsed, and the crowd let out a wail. Charlie, who I hadn't noticed was beside me, burst into noisy tears, and then I realized that the men who had gone inside a moment before, wearing safety helmets and fireproofs, had reappeared and that they were carrying something.

A stretcher with a person on it.

Charlie wailed again, and Alex put his arm round her, and I wondered vaguely where Will was, and my body thrilled with horror that someone was hurt.

Nobody was allowed anywhere near, but late-arriving parents who hadn't found their kids yet rushed the police manning the boundary, clamouring to see who they were pulling from the building. Kiaru squeezed my hand, and I squeezed his back, half hypnotized, glad and then guilty that everyone I cared about was accounted for.

Kes's hands moved from his mouth to cover his eyes, and people cried openly without seeming to know it. I didn't have a single properly formed thought until Kiaru nudged my arm, and told me it was five past nine.

'I have to get you back,' he said, as though I were a child or Cinderella, and I was too bewildered to protest.

More windows popped like gunshots and glass rained gold with fire, and Alisha was transfixed, resting her head on her mum's shoulder in the juddering firelight. She barely looked up as we said goodbye, and walking away from the heat, the way my and Kiaru's fingers wrapped round each other was no longer to do with romance. My teeth chattered all the way home.

Thirty-one

Sunshine flooded my windows, last night's storm forgotten, and Dad brought me a cup of tea, kissing my head like we were close again. It all came rushing back: the flames, the body, the firemen, ash from above.

'Have you heard anything?' I asked, and Dad held my hand.

'I'm sorry, Rosie. I'm afraid it was your teacher that you saw last night. It was Ms Chase.'

'What?'

'She's in hospital, apparently. I don't know any more than that. There's nothing concrete online yet. I'm going to walk down to get the paper. D'you want anything?'

I groaned into my pillow, nauseous. The day was going to be a difficult one, but I forced myself to sit up and face it. I needed to make friends with Ti, that was the first thing, and I wasn't going to let anyone stop me. Not even her. All this calamity put things in perspective. I would talk to Dad, like Kiaru said, and then walk round there and apologize. Maybe I could take a present . . . or Joey! She wouldn't be able to hate me if I had Joey with me. He was my secret weapon. The phone rang and then Dad shouted upstairs. 'Rosie? It's Fabio,' and his voice sounded odd because what was Fab doing calling me? A shock through my body, like an anchor dropping, and my heartbeat pounded in my ears. Had something happened to Ti?

I ran to where Dad stood holding the phone in the hallway, with an anxious expression.

'Rosie? Bella? That you?' Fab's frightened voice was like a pin in my neck.

'It's me.'

'Have you seen Titania? She didn't come home last night. She and her sister were meant to open up today but there's still no sign of them.'

I swallowed without meaning to. They didn't come home? What did he mean? They weren't allowed out. 'I haven't seen them.'

'No? Neither of them? Tell the truth, eh? We're worried sick. You won't get into trouble.'

'I haven't seen them.'

'You're sure?'

'I'm sorry, I wish I had. If Ti calls or anything I'll let you know.'

I'd barely put the phone down when I began shouting.

'Dad! I need my phone back *right now*! Ti's missing, I need to check my emails!'

'Keep your voice down!' Dad hissed. 'There's no need to panic your mum.'

'Phone and internet,' I demanded. I was done hiding things from Mum. She didn't get out of bed either way.

'What's happened?' Joey called, running down the attic stairs in his Superman onesie.

Dad pulled my mobile from his back pocket, muttering about how he'd been planning to let me have it back today because I'd been so mature this week. I snatched it from him, turning it on, watching impatiently as the screen loaded up.

'I'll get your computer,' he said, heading downstairs. 'Just calm down a bit. I'm sure Titania is fine.'

'Everything all right down there?' Mum shouted, and I called up that no, it wasn't, because Ti hadn't returned home since last night, and where else did she have to sleep, since she wasn't allowed to sleep over here any more?

'Do they think she's with Ophelia?' Dad said, returning with my laptop, but I didn't answer, just took it from him, and headed to my bedroom.

'They'll be up to something somewhere,' he said, and

his voice was so unworried it enraged me. 'They'll be fine, I promise you.'

'Oh, it's fine for Ti to be out all night, is it? So long as I'm not involved it doesn't matter?'

'Rosie, come on,' he pleaded, but I didn't have time to make him feel better.

'What's going on? Is Ti okay?' Joey asked, trailing me into my bedroom, his pyjamas so faded you could hardly tell which superhero he was supposed to be.

'I just need to see if she's been in touch,' I said as neutrally as I could.

Fat raindrops slapped against the window and I imagined Dad walking down the drive, pulling up the collar of his shirt, off to get the paper. I hoped he got soaked.

Wherever Ti was, let it be warm and dry.

As my emails and messages loaded I felt I would die with suspense.

Finally the list flashed up.

Eleven missed calls. One voice message.

All from Ti.

Thirty-two

'You have one, new, message. Received at eight, twenty-seven.'

Beeeeep.

'Rosie? Where are you? Why won't you answer? I really need you, Rose. Will your parents let me in if I come over? Ophelia's lost it. Will said the whole thing was a mistake, and Ophelia's blaming Dad, and I got in the way. I thought he was going to hit her again. He was – I can't . . . I can't believe what I'm saying . . . I'm so angry. I feel so . . . stupid, I never thought he'd do it to me. Oh my god, can you hear her? The police are going to be round in a minute . . . He's locked her in, and she's going crazy; she's smashing everything up. I don't know what to do. I'm scared. Oh my god, can you hear her? Ophelia! Ophelia, stop it! Please stop it. Oh god, Rosie, she's lost it. She's really lost it; she's broken in the head. Please answer your phone. I can't stay here.

I don't know what to do. I can't live here any more. I don't know where to go. Rosie, where are you? I need you. Where are you, Rosie? I really need—'

Beeeeep.

Thirty-three

Ti's mobile went straight to answerphone, and I guessed Fab and June still hadn't let her have it back. Her missed calls were all within minutes of each other on Friday evening from the landline. Her voice, babbling and frightened, made me cry.

Where was she? I felt responsible, like I'd lost her myself. Like she was something precious I could have carried in my pocket, which I'd forgotten to take care of.

I stroked Joey's hair for comfort as I played the message again. He had come in with his handheld computer, to sit beside me on the bed, and his thumbs clicked and clicked. He was the only one that hadn't lost faith in her, and I loved him for it.

My phone beeped, sending my fingers shaking as I begged the world and fate and gods that it was Ti.

But it was from a number I didn't have saved in my contacts.

NICE FRIENDS YOU'VE GOT. HIGH-FIVE TI FOR ME

The number ended 999, and I remembered: Charlie Fielding. Someone *not* to call in an emergency. I'd deleted her years ago, but she evidently hadn't deleted me.

NOT JUST STALKERS BUT KILLERS NOW TOO

Chase had died!? What was she talking about? It couldn't be true. I breathed in the clean, soapy smell of Joey's hair, trying not to freak out, but my heartbeat was like something outside of my body, like being walloped with a stick every other second. Ti had started the fire? Is that what Charlie meant? It wasn't possible. But Ophelia . . .

Last time Will had dumped her, she'd thrown a book he'd bought her through his bedroom window. It was the Philip Pullman trilogy, a thick dark green hardback, and it had smashed straight through. Ophelia had got her first caution from the police and was banned from ever going round there again, even though she'd been friends on-and-off with Charlie for years.

That whole cracked night Ti had followed her sister around, unable to talk her down or get her home, but unwilling to leave either. She'd been with her every second, witnessed every moment, and when I asked why she hadn't stopped her, she'd got mad.

188

'I couldn't, obviously,' she said. '*Obviously* I tried.'

But Charlie hadn't said Ophelia. She'd said Ti. I wanted to call Fab back, but less than two minutes had passed since we had spoke and I was so angry with him for hurting Ti that I didn't know what I'd say. My legs itched and my heart juddered. I had to do something.

I still knew Charlie's home number off by heart.

There were a few rings, then someone answered; only it wasn't someone answering, but a snooty recording asking me to leave my details.

'I need a lift!' I called out, putting my phone in my pocket, and dashing upstairs to where a damp Dad was whispering with Mum. 'Dad? *Please.* I need a lift.'

I was half shouting, half crying, and Dad stood straight away, scooping his keys off the *Flushing Packet*, which lay open on the bed. FIRE AT FAIRFIELDS was the headline. Mum squeezed his hand, and he leant down to kiss her cheek.

'Come *on*,' I said, unable to appreciate the moment of affection between them in my panic.

Thirty-four

Will Fielding knew something. He had to. I bit at my lip, wishing Dad would go faster as we drove along Castle Road, noticing traces of the storm Kiaru and me had watched coming in. A tree had fallen near the castle car park, and there were leaves and twigs all over the road. At the top of the hill, where the cliff was too steep for houses, police tape covered a huge hole in the trees and hedgerow.

'Jesus,' Dad said.

A car had gone over the edge of the cliff. Black skids marked the road and splintered trunks showed their milky insides. Dad didn't slow down, and I knew we were both thinking of Ti.

I avoided looking at Kiaru's house as we approached Charlie and Will's, tried not to remember his kiss and how I'd liquefied, because where had Ti been then? Calling my mobile again and again? I didn't allow myself even a glance. Until I knew Ti was safe I wouldn't think of him.

The Fieldings' house was buttery yellow brick with huge feature windows and a balcony along the front, and Sophie was unpacking shopping from their gold Mitsubishi in the drive when we pulled in. Looking to see who had arrived, her expression fell, as though she had expected someone more important.

'Rosie!' she called, recovering fast. 'How are you holding up? Dreadful news about Ms Chase this morning, isn't it? Did you hear? She took a turn for the worse, and they've moved her into intensive care. She went in to try to save something, silly woman, and got trapped inside. It was touch and go for a moment there. Char is beside herself. She's buying a card and flowers as we speak. We were there when the firemen pulled her out, you know. Unrecognizable. Poor woman.'

Dad gave Sophie a severe look, but she was oblivious. Relief flooded through me that Chase was alive, and I sent up thanks as Sophie shouted to Will.

'Empty the boot of shopping please, as well, before you disappear upstairs again,' she said coldly, as Will appeared, looking confused to see my face. 'Mimi's almost here.'

At the name I had a flash of Charlie's grandmother: linen suits and backcombed hair. At one of Charlie's sleepovers years ago she'd shouted 'sex' when taking our photo, and Charlie, Mia and me had fallen about laughing. I still had a copy of the picture somewhere, the three of us leaning on each other and hysterical in pastel pyjamas. A different me.

'I won't stand any more bother on account of you today, young man.'

Will closed his eyes slowly, as though one more word from his mother might make them burst from his head, and he seemed tense, unlike the way he was at school. He had a cut across his right cheek, and a fat lip, and his hair was more like a banana pancake than a Mr Whippy. He held himself very straight like he'd never met me, though we'd spent hours together as kids.

'What's up?' he said, and I saw scratches on his neck too, as though he'd fallen from a tree, though you couldn't imagine him climbing one. He didn't bother to hide the fact that he wanted me to leave.

'Have you seen Ophelia?' I said, and Will's eyes flicked over my shoulder, spooked.

'*Christ's sake,*' he hissed. 'Don't mention that name round here. Her dad only just left; he was up here shouting his mouth off again. Mum nearly had to call the police.'

Dad's engine hummed at the end of the drive, and I could see him through the windshield, listening to Sophie with a grim expression.

'So you haven't seen her?'

'Not since last night, no. Why does everyone keep asking me that? She was going off on one before the show. Usual craziness.'

He stepped out from the doorstep to begin unloading the boot, like he didn't want me examining him too closely. I hadn't talked to him one-on-one for years, and I might have been intimidated if I couldn't remember him as a little boy. He was a total show-off like Charlie, always singing or dancing or clowning around. Once, when he was eight or nine, he'd shown us how a boy could hide his willy between his legs so it looked like he was a girl. Following him to the car now, I held that in my mind, refusing to be discouraged by his unfriendliness.

'What happened to your face?'

'I walked into a door.'

'Pffff. What about the scratches on your neck?'

'The cat did it; she never learned to put her claws in.'

'Will, I know you were a couple.'

'We were not a *couple*. The girl's delusional.'

'Well, you were something.'

'What's with all the amateur sleuthing all of a sudden? Is it the latest craze for teenage girls?'

'Look, I don't care about you and Ophelia, I'm worried about Ti.'

'The whole family's insane. Bloody Italians. Don't know how I ever put up with her.'

He breathed slowly out of his nose in a way I

associated with Kiaru's dusty attic room and meditation. He was nervous.

Sophie breezed past us, smelling of soap and perfume. She ruffled my hair as she passed, and I realized Charlie must never have told her about the gravy incident after all. 'We all miss you round here, Rosie. Come up and see us one day, hey? This fire's been a real blow for Char, right in the middle of the finale too. You know what a sucker she is for the spotlight, and she *adores* Ms Chase. She could do with a friend, someone understanding and kind like you . . . Someone who'll bring out her softer side.'

Her voice changed to businesslike as she shifted her attention to Will.

'You can put it all away as well please, William. And don't go anywhere because we're all sitting down for lunch, no arguments.'

Sophie headed up the stairs, and Will pulled the last bags from the boot, shaking his head.

'You seem like you're acting very strange to me, Will. I think you know something. Ti and Ophelia didn't go home last night, neither of them, and I got two weird text messages off your sister this morning.'

'She thinks Ti started the fire, that's why. She reckons she saw her on school grounds or something. Probably another smear campaign. Girls are mental.'

'Just call me if you hear anything, that's all I want. I won't get you into trouble. I'm just looking for Ti.'

194

He looked at me like I was mental too, then walked into the house laden with shopping.

'No good?' Dad said, as I threw myself against the passenger seat, then struggled with my seat belt.

He put the car into reverse. 'What awful news about your teacher, Rosie. I'm sorry Sophie sprang it on you like that; we wanted to tell you about the latest developments a bit more gently.'

I didn't know what to say. I couldn't think about it yet. How was she doing? And what had she been going in to save?

'I'm sure she'll be all right,' he said, though he didn't sound sure at all. Times like this I wished my dad was better at performing.

We pulled out of the Fieldings' drive and on to Castle Road, and I closed my eyes so I wouldn't have to be reminded by Kiaru's house of how badly I'd deserted Ti. Had she really been on school grounds last night? We must have missed each other by seconds.

'Those tyre tracks we saw were to do with Sophie, apparently. Someone stole her car, joyriders, she reckons, 'cause the keys were still in her handbag.'

I could feel him examining me, and I bet he wanted to ask if Ti or Ophelia knew how to hotwire a vehicle.

'You look pale, Rosie. It is a bit much, this, isn't it? Let's get you home, eh?'

'This never would have happened if you hadn't kept us apart,' I said very quietly.

'*Rosie,*' Dad said, reaching for my hand, but I crossed my arms tight across my chest, staring blindly out the passenger window. The car stayed where it was for a few seconds, poised on Castle Road, about to drive off, and I could feel Dad looking at me, but I wouldn't turn his way.

'Ti's dad hit her last night, and she wanted to come over. But she didn't know if she was allowed,' I said, staring at the fir trees around Will's house. 'If anything's happened to her, I'll never forgive you.'

I wouldn't forgive myself either, but I wasn't going to tell him that.

Behind us a car beeped, and Dad lifted the clutch. The tiny green fingers of the fir trees rippled in the wind, and I squeezed my arms to my ribcage.

Will was hiding something, it was obvious. All I had to do was find out what.

Thirty-five

Joey was waiting at the kitchen table for us when we got back. He looked up when we arrived, thumbs flicking wildly over his handheld computer.

'Mum says to go straight up,' he said, his game pausing with a ping.

'You stay here, Joe. Finish your go,' Dad said, and that was when I really felt it because Dad never encouraged Joey to play computer games; he was expecting the worst too. 'Actually make us all a cup of tea, eh? I'll give you a quid.'

'My rates have gone up with inflation, that will be one pound fifty in total,' Joey said, without looking from his screen.

'Don't push it, Joe,' Dad snapped.

Joey slapped his computer down on his lap, blue eyes drilling into Dad's and his mouth working, but I could hardly pay attention to him. I was struggling myself.

When had it become so hard to untie plimsolls? My fingers trembled, and I couldn't get a handle on the laces.

'Here,' Dad said, bending down to undo them for me.

Joey gawped at me like I was trying to pull my actual feet off. A feeling of catastrophe had covered me, and I couldn't shake it. Walking up the stairs, I made promises to myself and the world and Ti. If she was all right, I would always face up to things. If she was all right, I'd stop telling lies. Most of all, if she was all right, I'd be a better friend. I wouldn't abandon her again.

As soon as I saw Mum's face I knew my fear was founded.

'Sit down,' she said, patting the bed, and Dad took my hand automatically, as though he were the one delivering the news, and I realized that whatever it was he knew already.

'I'm so sorry, Rosie . . . Ti's and Ophelia's clothes have been found on the beach at Durgan. Their wallets were there. Money, bank cards. Everything.'

I was shaking my head, and I wished Joey was here, because I needed someone to be brave for.

'There was a bottle of whisky nearby, half empty. The police think they might have drunk it and gone for a swim . . . I'm so sorry, baby, it looks like they might have got into trouble. Come here. Come here. It's okay. It's okay. Shhhhh.'

I heard cups rattling on a tray and then Joey's voice trembling as he asked what had happened. Dad whispered to Joey, and I knew he must be afraid but I couldn't look up from where I'd buried my face in the crook of Mum's neck. It was hot and wet from my tears, but I couldn't let go.

Mum held her me-free arm out, and Joey burrowed in for a cuddle while she whispered in his ear. I don't know what Dad was doing, but Joey held my hand.

'Ti's all right,' he said after a few minutes of this, though he looked panicked as he spoke. 'She's a strong swimmer.'

'She is,' I said, because it was true. I loved my little brother.

'We don't know anything for sure yet, Joe,' Dad said in the tone he used when he was trying to discourage him from getting his hopes up, and I felt bitterness creep through my blood like a disease. If they hadn't taken my phone, I could have helped her.

Climbing off the bed, everything seemed uncertain suddenly: my legs, the world, my life.

'Where you going, Rosie? Don't be on your own,' Mum said.

I stumbled down the stairs, misjudging the distance and number of steps and twisting my ankle. Dad called to see if I was all right but I ignored him. Let him think I was hurt. I was. More than I could explain.

Lying in the sunlight at the end of my bed, I tried to pick through all the new information, but I couldn't get it straight. Ti wasn't dead. She couldn't be. She'd called me last night. I'd heard her voice!

If Ti were dead I'd feel it, like an earthquake. I'd feel it psychically, and I didn't.

Joey was right: she was a good swimmer. She loved and respected the sea. She'd never go into rough water like that at Durgan, no matter how upset or drunk she was. Never. But then why had her clothes and wallet been found? And where was she?

Thirty-six

Rumours about Ti were everywhere. I didn't want to listen, but couldn't help it. Charlie said she'd seen her stumbling at the edges of school grounds with a bottle of whisky when she was getting fresh air before going onstage for Act Two. Ti must have started the fire, people said. Who else would it be?

Charlie thought that the twins had killed themselves, like Thelma and Louise, to escape the consequences of their actions, but the police reckoned they were only skinny-dipping drunk and had got into trouble by mistake. But it was so cold that night, who in their right minds would skinny dip?

Liliana, the postwoman, swore she'd seen the girls in the Fieldings' car on Castle Road, that it must've spun off the road shortly after because of the winds.

Nobody was welcome near me except for Joey.

I reread Ti's emails, wincing at how dishonest I'd been

in mine. Complaining about Mum's illness and how hard everything was when really I was obsessing over Kiaru, and having a laugh with Alisha. I'd been so angry with Ophelia when she accused me of using Mum's illness as an excuse to be selfish, but she had been right.

I noticed the times on hers. How long it had taken me to reply, and how quickly she had responded. She obviously hadn't been sleeping, or not well. She must have felt so lonely. And then I'd gotten Leon's name wrong, the boy with the wet lips who smacked her on the back of the head. No wonder she hadn't wanted to be my friend. The ones before the milkshake shop were worst of all. I read them from between my fingers, like I was watching a horror film. How must she have felt when she saw me? And what had I been running from?

A terror I could hardly interact with was that Ophelia had thrown herself in the water, in a fit of madness, and Ti had been pushed under as she tried to save her. But why the piles of clothes? And if the girls *had* started the fire, and were hiding somewhere, what were they wearing?

I wanted to read the messages aloud to my dad, but I couldn't talk to him yet. His protests were all about equality and giving people a fair chance, but he hadn't managed to do that with Ti. He preferred me to be friends with kids like Alisha and Kiaru, with perfect manners and rich parents.

All Mum cared about was marks. It didn't matter who I was friends with so long as they were swots. She would prefer me to be miserable and tagging along with mean old Charlie Fielding if it meant I got more As.

Worst of all was that I'd listened. I'd let them convince me when I should have been convincing them.

Kiaru rang, but I didn't want to talk to him. I only wanted to speak to Ti, and it was never her calling.

The only thing more impossible than sleeping was lying awake with these thoughts, and so one night, I dressed in black, and slipped out the back door into the darkness.

Thirty-seven

But it wasn't as easy as that. Nightwandering was terrifying when you were on your own, and after walking a hundred metres along the coast path I sprinted back to the road with its lovely lamp posts and pavement and occasional car. The sky was clear and full of stars, but they only emphasized how small I was. How vulnerable. I took deep breaths and tried again, cursing myself for not bringing a torch.

The thing was that Ti hated them, and I'd got out of the habit. She complained about light pollution and how they ruined your night vision, getting mad every time I turned mine on, and in the end it was easier to just follow her as she stomped along, breaking into a run occasionally when she got excited.

'It's an exercise in faith!' she shouted back to me, as I ordered her to slow down or better still come back.

'Faith in what?'

'In yourself and your senses! In the coast path!'

So many times she nearly fell over, but she never grew cautious. She'd trip and whoop and then I'd hear her laughing. 'That was a close one!'

'I've got the best night vision in the world,' she said another time, as we lay on Durgan Beach, watching the stars. We tested it by seeing who'd lose sight of a satellite trundling across the sky first.

'I can still see it,' we said.

'I can still see it,' she said.

Until I had to admit defeat.

Shaking my terror away, I tried again, imagining Ti striding ahead of me. I found a big stick, and held it in front of me like a staff. I would defend myself against spirits and fate and murderers. Against my own fear. No more running away. Focusing on my breathing, I forced myself to walk on, away from the lights of the road, allowing my night vision to kick in. The hedge looked like fingers and claws, and cobwebs swept my face, but I pushed forward, telling myself I was brave until I almost was.

Something good happened when the two of us walked together, and I tried to find it by myself. I focused on the little thunder rushes of the sea, the salt air on my face and in my lungs. I let my thoughts float freely, never getting stuck. You are safe you are safe you are safe. One step at a time, until I'd walked so far the pads of my feet burned.

Gradually, I relaxed. Ti wasn't with me, but we'd explored these places together so completely it felt like she was. Memories engulfed me. I headed west towards Swanpool and the golf course to check Daphne's bench, an old meeting place of ours. The seat was named after DAPHNE, WHO LOVED THE SEA, and we argued over who was more Daphne. I said it was me because I always photographed the water, but Ti said it was her because she knew about the actual ecosystems.

'You only like it as a picture,' she said, as I focused the waves through my new camera. 'The sea's just an idea to you, a surface image. You don't care about the world that's underneath.' Was that true?

I touched Kiaru's gate as I passed, growled at Charlie's. Remembering Will earlier, I lifted the catch, and pushed, staring into the dark of their garden. I could hear the water of the fountain bubbling in their huge pond, could see its froth catching the moonlight.

'Titania,' I whispered.

Inside the house, one of their Dalmatians started barking, then another, and I rushed back to the coast path.

Daphne's bench was set a little way off the steep track down to Durgan Beach, and the ocean grew loud as I approached. Of course there was nobody there, just me. I sat with a heavy feeling, remembering the years before Ti came, when I was still trying to fit in with Charlie and Mia, before Ti showed me that singing competitions

206

and ranking each other's hair and smiles and dance moves weren't the best ways to spend your time.

The cruise ships on the horizon were lit up like birthday cakes, and I thought of Ti and Ophelia's party at the café last summer. They'd bickered about what sort of cake June should make, only agreeing on a mermaid if she could have straight hair like Ophelia's, in spite of the fact that every mermaid in the history of the world had wavy hair like Ti's.

That was making a deal with Ophelia. Your forty-nine to her fifty-one was as close as you got.

Heading to Swanpool I stopped at the meadow where I had tried to teach Ti to play Frisbee when she first arrived. My second throw had hit her in the face and made her nose bleed, and we'd had to run all the way to the toilet block at Swanpool to get some tissue. By the time we arrived she looked like a victim of crime with blood all over her T-shirt and teeth and hands, and when she was cleaned up the man at the tea stall gave us both a free ice cream.

Staring at the spot where we had stood all those years ago I caught sight of the Petrified Lady, a skull-sized rock with an eerily human expression by the hedge that I hadn't thought about for years. Ti and me had lifted the lichen-covered boulder once, and found an ancient-looking turquoise-tinged penny underneath. After that, if we had an embarrassing or personal question, we would ask the Penny of Old who was all-seeing and non-judgemental.

Would Ti ever become a deep-sea diver? Would I ever need a bra?

Tails for yes, heads for no.

What had happened to the Penny of Old, and why did I never hold on to things? The Petrified Lady was damp and green, desperate for the summer to warm her through, and lifting her I felt dizzy with a hope I couldn't quite understand. Until I saw it.

The penny.

My stomach twisted and I heard myself gasp as two thoughts hit me consecutively.

Ti was alive! Ti was in trouble.

We had once planned how we could use the penny to communicate if we were ever in peril. Ti loved all that Famous Five code stuff, and was for ever dreaming of adventure. Heads up was a heads up. It meant 'Come save me. I'm doomed'. Head's down meant 'Relax, I'm well. Have a cup of tea'.

The queen's details were dull from being in the dark for years, but I could make out her nose and crown. It was a head's up.

The penny was cold in my fist. Was this the last thing Ti had touched? I sent up a prayer that she was okay, and asked the Penny of Old (and the Petrified Lady, if she had any powers) to bring her back to me. I daren't ask a direct question in case I got a no, and so I kissed the queen's icy nose, soil dotting my lips, and placed her face down beneath the stone.

My instinct told me to check Daphne's bench again, and I headed in its direction, heart whacking. Hope bubbled in me. Maybe Ti had left the penny as a test, to see if I truly cared about her or not. Maybe she was at Daphne's bench right now, and we would hug, and she would tell me this perfectly obvious story explaining where she'd been this whole time, clearing up all the rumours, and we'd be sisters again.

Because the last time I saw her couldn't be *the last time I saw her*. The memories in my head couldn't be the only ones. I needed new memories, for her to do fresh and brilliant and embarrassing things. To get it wrong and upset me and get it right and make me brave and be herself. For us to walk.

Gorse, gorse and hawthorn: my thighs burned from the hill, and I wasn't breathing any more. Let her be sitting, watching the horizon, hoping I cared enough to understand her sign.

But Daphne's bench was empty.

I sat, damp from the rain, surrounded by debris – Monster Munch packet, KitKat foil, piece of hose pipe – wiping water from my face. Sea mist, drizzle, tears. What did it matter? Ti was gone.

Thirty-eight

I woke, sweating, from dreams of tsunamis at Fairfields to find Joey by my bed, looking at me as though he didn't know who I was. I screwed my eyes shut.

Pots had accumulated in my room: last night's bowl, dried-out bread, a spoon smearing soup on the carpet. I'd heard Mum and Dad whisper about me while I pretended to sleep – Mum: 'We were too hard on her.' Dad: 'She'll be fine' – but getting out of bed felt like an old habit I couldn't return to.

'I saw your eye whites,' Joey whined, frustrated, and something touched my nose. It smelt of chocolate and had foil that crinkled, and I couldn't resist a peek.

'Eye whites,' he said again matter-of-factly. In his favourite double-denim outfit with matching blue socks and Mum's gold wolf brooch on his collar he was rolling a Kinder egg over my face. He held it out to me, and I peeled the foil off, split the chocolate in half, and put the toy-filled egg in my mouth. Joey watched in horror until I blew the unopened orange capsule across the room, and then he laugh-shrieked so manically that I felt bad.

The capsule hit the radiator with a clanging sound and Joey went to retrieve it. He wrapped his arms round my neck, and I wanted him to keep them there forever. I wished he was small again so I could carry him around with me, my own personal monkey. I breathed in his soapy, salty, little-boy smell.

'Kiaru called again while you were asleep,' he said, pulling away from me, and climbing on to the bed as my heart crash-banged, cheeks burning up.

'I told him you were ill.'

'Good boy.'

'But you're not.' Joey stood over me, his feet trapping me in the duvet and began to bounce. 'So get up.'

'No.'

'Get *up.*' He pulled at my duvet, and I clutched it to my neck.

'Get out if you're going to be like this.'

His face turned naughty and his fists gripped the material, and I could see how much he wanted to pull it from me.

'You'll never win,' I said. 'Think of Leg Wars.'

He glared at me, and his breathing was fast.

'I defeat you in every physical battle, and you know it!'

His knuckles returned to their normal colour.

'Just be on my side, Joe,' I said. 'Just for a bit longer.'

He sighed, disappointed, but his face returned to my favourite version of itself, and he lifted the covers at the end of the bed, and tucked himself in by my feet.

At lunchtime Dad came to ask if I'd deliver the lasagne he'd baked round to the De Furias, but I couldn't face it. I used a bad stomach as an excuse, which wasn't a lie, because it physically pained me to think about Ti's parents by now. What must they think of me?

Dad looked disappointed, so I told him it should have been a cottage pie or something English, because he could never beat Fab's lasagne, and when he shrugged that off, saying everyone appreciated a home-cooked meal, I asked if he didn't feel like a bit of a hypocrite, acting so concerned about the De Furias now, when for weeks he'd been trying to cut them from our lives.

He didn't answer that, just left the room, which was what I wanted. Why hadn't he been more interested when it would have helped? Why hadn't I? It was too little too late, and it made me feel worse.

But Dad wouldn't give up. 'They're organizing a candle-lit vigil at Durgan,' he told me later, when he came home for lunch. 'This Friday. We'll meet where the girls' clothes were found, and light a candle. June's going to sing, and Fab's going to speak. Nice idea, isn't it? I said they could borrow my speakers and PA if they want.

'June was very clear about it: it's a candlelit vigil, not a memorial. "Every flame that flickers will be a symbol of hope." That's what she said.'

I pulled the quilt over my head, and waited for him to leave.

'You've got to get up,' Joey said, when I was still in bed at three o'clock the next day, and I knew he was frightened. Mum hadn't been out of bed since last Monday when she overheard the Awful Thing in the kitchen, and no matter how many times I told him Joey refused to believe CFS wasn't contagious. I couldn't tell him I was walking at night, because he was loose with secrets – he didn't understand why they needed to exist.

'I can't get up, Joe; I feel too bad. I left her on her own, and now it's too late. I was too selfish and now I've lost her.'

He looked around the room for a minute, and I wished he was older so he could understand properly or reassure me in a way that I could believe.

'You're being selfish again now,' he said. 'But you can stop it. You just have to get up and come out with me.'

'Wow,' I said, because he was right. He was only eight, but he was right. 'You're a little wise man.'

'I know.'

Within the hour I was out of bed, showered and dressed, and walking Joey into town to buy Mum a get-well card and some sweets.

Thirty-nine

Suddenly the whole town cared about the De Furia twins. Posters were displayed in every shop window – Ti and Ophelia beaming at their birthday party last year, with their straight-haired mermaid cake. Ti loved the cake so much she kept the green glittery candles. She was soppy like that. The conch shell I'd found on Durgan Beach last spring tide was still on her dressing table with some sea glass in it. She still had the ticket from the aquarium for Joey's birthday.

Joey treated the posters like adverts for a band the sisters were in, pointing them out and cheering them, and I tried to channel some of his faith that they were happy somewhere. Kids from school smiled sombrely at me when we passed. Proximity to tragedy breeds popularity it would seem.

'This is *awesome*,' Joey said as the second group of girls from my school cooed over how cute he looked in his blue best.

We were picking out a card in Wilkos when I saw them: Charlie, Alex and Mia, scooping sweets into pink-striped paper bags. I questioned Joey's card choice, sending him back to search again, hoping we might dodge them if we wasted extra minutes. Instead of chivvying him along as usual, I indulged his quest to compile Mum the ultimate bag of pick-and-mix, languidly debating the perfect chocolate to jelly sweet ratio.

Still, walking out on to the high street, there they were.

Charlie made a beeline for me, and the others followed. She lifted her hand for a high-five from Joey, as though we were still friendly, but he left her hanging.

'Is that for Ms Chase?' she asked, tapping the get-well-soon card that Joey hugged to his chest. 'Because she's not allowed visitors yet.'

Joey opened his mouth, but I glared at him to shut him up. The gossip machine wouldn't get any new information from us.

'So she isn't dead then?' I said, and Charlie looked embarrassed.

'She almost was! She slipped into a coma. It didn't look good!'

Part of her was enjoying this, I could tell. 'You should delete my number from your phone. I deleted you years ago.'

'Don't be nasty, Rosie, not with what's going on. I got swept along with everything that's been happening, that's all. It was a mistake. Have you been to pay your respects?'

Kids had been taking flowers to the burnt-out Drama block, but I didn't want to see. It sounded like a depressing and weird thing to do, but mostly I didn't want to hear the rumours flying around. Mia drew closer, unable to resist the pull of whatever might happen next, but Alex hung back. Maybe the idea of Ophelia drowning had made him develop some empathy.

'You should go. See it for yourself,' Charlie said. She bit her lip and frowned. 'What *happened* to them? Why did they do it?'

'Nothing happened to them,' Joey said, when it became clear I wasn't going to answer. 'And they didn't *do* anything.'

Adoring looks appeared on Mia's and Charlie's faces, but Joey didn't smile. He hated people finding him cute when he was being serious. He continued to talk, as though giving a statement to the press.

'They've just gone off somewhere for a bit. For a break. There's really no reason at all to worry.' He puffed out his chest and held Charlie's gaze.

Alex was staring at the ground, which surprised me, because Mia was looking from me to Charlie like we were daytime TV.

'Will went to see Ms Chase yesterday. He's allowed in, because they're so close. She's still in intensive care. Her room is full of flowers.'

'He's livid about what happened,' Mia added, eager to say anything Will-related.

'She's not well enough to talk,' Charlie said. 'I don't know if she knows about Ti and Ophelia yet . . .'

'That they started the fire?' Mia said.

'Nobody knows who set the fire,' Joey said.

'I meant that they're . . . missing. The police were round there again yesterday,' Charlie added.

'Everyone's saying their dad did it,' Mia said.

'Did what? Nothing has been *done* to anyone,' I said, gesturing with my eyes to Joey whose face had dropped, and the fierceness in my voice broke through Mia's and Charlie's scandal-crazed pea brains.

'There was a *huge* argument the night before they went missing, that's all I'm saying. Everyone says that the neighbours complained,' Charlie said.

Without having to think, I was on Fab's side. He had the De Furia temper, and he lashed out, but he adored his girls.

'Who's "everyone"?' I said.

'People that know.'

'You mean your parents and your brother?'

Charlie twitched her hair from her face in a haughty little gesture.

'Tell Will to stop spreading lies to cover his own back.'

'What are you talking about? He hated Ophelia.'

'Sure,' I said. 'He hated her. That's why they used to meet in secret all the time. To *hate* each other.'

Charlie looked fuming, and Mia's smile dropped. She had been mooning over Will for as long as I had known her. Alex looked like he didn't want to be here at all, and I wondered if Ti had been right when she claimed he was still in love with Ophelia.

'They haven't met in secret for months,' Charlie said.

'So how come Fab came round your house the day after they went missing? And what was "the huge fight" he had with Ophelia about?'

Charlie's blue eyes flicked to the side for a second, doubtful.

'Fab's a mad man,' she said, recovering. 'Everyone knows. The whole family are insane.'

'I expect the police will want to talk to Will soon too,' I said. 'Seeing as he hated her so much, and that they spent so much time together . . .'

Charlie's head was shaking, and I felt sorry for her, because she was such a spiteful person, and her life was really going to suck if she carried on this way. Joey looked at me to check everything was okay, and I ruffled his hair to reassure him.

'Hurts when rumours start about the people you love, doesn't it?' I said, and putting my arm round Joey, I pushed through them, and it was strange to imagine that I'd ever felt intimidated. They were petty and malicious and small.

'Ti will come back soon, won't she?' Joey said, and I nodded.

'She will.'

Faux-scolding him for taking all the best sweets before we delivered them to Mum, I took the road that led to the De Furia café, praying it would be open. Business as usual would mean they had faith that their daughters were safe and well, and coming back. But it was shut. No note on the door or anything.

Poor Fab. He had enough to worry about without stories like that going round. How were he and June coping? I tried to imagine how Dad would feel if things were the other way round, and my heart ached.

At home I sent my brother upstairs with the treats for Mum, then headed back out again, up the hill to the Beacon. It didn't matter if it was awkward at the De Furias' house, I realized. What mattered was that I let them know I cared enough about them and their daughters to go and see how they were doing.

Forty

The curtains in the living room and the bedroom upstairs were closed, and it took me a minute to build the nerve to knock. Perhaps they didn't want guests. Perhaps they were having difficulty sleeping, and making up for it this afternoon. What if I ruined their first deep sleep since . . . I rapped on the door, hard enough to sting my knuckles before I could wimp out.

Movement inside, and then Fab appeared, thick grey hair seeming to swarm around one side of his head, his broad face frosted with white stubble. He wore old jeans and a sweater, rather than his usual shirt and checked trousers, and on his feet were the oldest, most beat-up and dirty-looking slippers I'd ever seen.

'Rosie,' he said gruffly, returning into the house in a way that I hoped meant I should follow. At the end of the dark hallway June peered cautiously from the kitchen.

'Rosa!' she said, and a smile broke out on her face. Her calling me 'Rosa' gave me strength, and I looked each of them in the eye.

'I want to help,' I said, and June nodded gladly, as though she had been expecting this. She wore a dressing gown too, with an old-fashioned nightie underneath, like someone's grandma from a programme about the Victorians. She had on thick slouchy socks that pooled round her ankles as though considering falling off altogether.

'Coffee?' Fab said, taking apart the small aluminium coffee maker that all the De Furias used. I preferred the jar stuff, but Fab refused to have it in the house.

'Yes please.'

'Sit down,' June said, following her own instructions. Fab shook coffee into his little contraption and set it on the hob, then took a cigarette from a packet on the windowsill, and stepped out the back door to smoke. June didn't take her eyes off me. Usually it was Fab that did the talking – he liked to grill people, asking questions and poking fun, not caring about being polite – but today he didn't have anything to say.

'It's lovely to see you,' June said. 'I've been wanting to get in touch.'

The coffee on the hob began to stir, and Fab blew out a stream of smoke using more power than seemed strictly necessary. He was like Ophelia in that respect. Cigarette smoke drifted into the room, mixing with the coffee smell, and I was reminded of dozens of early breakfasts here, before Ti's shift started on Saturdays and Sundays.

'Did you hear from Ti? Before . . . ?' She let her sentence trail off, and blinked, and I jumped in to fill the gap, not wanting to finish that thought either.

'I got an answerphone message, but I didn't hear it till the next day. I got suspended from school, and Dad took my phone, you see. Plus we'd sort of fell out. I had some missed calls,' I said vaguely, and then changed my mind: 'Eleven. She needed me and I wasn't there.'

June nodded. Clearly she understood that. 'And what did she say?' she asked, and I felt my face burning up. June seemed different to usual. More formidable and alert. More like her daughters.

'It was a bit garbled, but she said there'd been an argument,' I said hesitantly. June winced, and Fab took a deep drag on his cigarette, then scraped it down the brickwork before chucking it over next-door's fence. June didn't look at him, but lowered her head slightly, and I tried to remember if Ti had said her mum was there too.

'I hit her,' Fab announced, walking to where the coffee hissed on the hob.

He pulled a cupboard door open, retrieved three gold-tipped china cups, and began pouring expertly without spilling a drop. There were dark rings around

223

his eyes, and his mouth was very straight. 'I hit my littlest girl.'

June looked at him now, and her eyes were accusing and angry, and I realized that since I'd arrived they hadn't talked directly to each other.

Fab put my cup in front of me. Shaking his head, he tipped spoonfuls of sugar into his and June's coffees, then pushed the bowl over to me. Wiping his hands over his face, he sniffed, then drank his coffee in two quick, loud slurps. He put the delicate cup on the table, and all the time June eyed him with the same unforgiving expression.

'That what it said in the message?' he asked, and he seemed boyish in his slippers and T-shirt, this big man whose shouts I'd listened to since I could remember.

I nodded.

'You girls tell each other everything, don't you? Have the police spoken to you? They might want to . . .'

I shook my head fast, wanting him and June to know that this wasn't what I believed. Fab could be scary and unpredictable, but he was warm too, telling jokes and teasing. Once at dinner when Ophelia was being a brat, he draped linguine around her head, like a pasta crown. It shocked her so much her bad mood evaporated instantly.

'Why haven't they been round?' June said, standing up. 'I'm going to call PC Rush. They should be talking to everyone, it's like they've given up . . .'

Fab carried on as though June hadn't spoken. 'I just thought, if we could keep them out of trouble these years, we'd be okay. Just be tough until they were old enough to make good choices . . .'

Fab turned his cup, and June walked to the dresser to get something from a drawer.

'It's hard being the father of beautiful girls,' he said. 'When you know what boys are like. And they don't listen to you. They don't listen to their father like they should . . .'

'Look, Rosie,' June said. 'They found this on the beach, with their clothes.'

In her hand was the seahorse necklace I'd bought for her fifteenth birthday.

'The chain's broken,' I said, as she placed the delicate gold in my palm.

June nodded sadly. 'She loved that necklace.'

What had happened? Had she pulled it off? Why? June and me stared at the tiny charm, as Fab went out for another cigarette.

'My brother thinks they're hiding,' I said.

'They're punishing him,' June said, without lowering her voice.

'They'll not come back,' Fab called in from the garden.

'De Furias are stubborn,' June admitted. 'But they're loyal too.'

'Cut off our tongue in spite of our mouths.'

225

I couldn't help a tiny smile at the Fabism.

'There's no way Ti would swim at Durgan unless she knew it was safe,' I said.

'See!' June's face brightened. 'Fabio's finding it hard to think positive. He doesn't know the meaning of P. M. A.' She turned to look at him properly for the first time since I'd got there. 'Positive. Mental. Attitude.'

Fab jutted out his chin, returning to the table.

'We've had a lot of time to think,' June said, and Fab looked at his empty cup, turned it ninety degrees.

'We got things wrong, worked them too hard. Didn't let them have enough freedom. It's a lesson, I'm sure of it. These last few days have been awful, but what did we expect? We put them in a cage. Expected too much. I should have been on their side more. No, Fab! I should. They needed me.'

June's cheeks were flushed and she talked fast, and I remembered the mean impressions Ti used to do of her mild, walked-over mum. How surprised she'd be to see her now. Her voice was husky like Ti's, but her face was all Ophelia: big eyes and high cheeks and full lips. She was overcome with feeling, and Fab put his hand over hers.

'It's an emotional time,' he said. 'We're thinking very hard about what we could have done different. Expect you are too . . . We're thinking to sell the café. We don't want it no more. They hated that place. *The effing café*

226

they called it. Funny really, because we got it for them. We wanted to give them opportunities, but maybe they were too young. You can't force people, can you?'

We sat for a while longer, drinking another round of coffee, and talking about the vigil, and nobody mentioned the fire, or Chase, or Will, and I was glad. It felt like sitting together, without the girls, was all we could cope with in that moment. As I was leaving, after giving me an uncomfortably long hug, June pressed the necklace into my hand.

'Keep it,' she said. 'And pray for her to come back.'

When it was time to leave, and after June finally let me go, Fab escorted me to the door.

'You've surprised me, coming round here, talking like this. I thought you were a little—' he poked his bottom lip out, searching, and June put her hand on his arm, just above the elbow.

'Weak,' he said.

June squeezed my hand. 'This is Fab talking, Rosie, not me . . .'

'We did! What's the matter? I'm giving her a compliment. Ti always loved you, *Rosie, Rosie, Rosie,* and I couldn't see it – always so quiet, no stories to tell – but I'm getting it now. It's a different way, you have. Gentle. Like my Junebug.'

He pulled his wife to him, and in spite of her nerves, and the circumstances, she flushed with pleasure.

'There's different ways to be strong, and it takes all kinds. You're a good friend,' he said, and I had to wipe my eyes again, which pleased him.

'That's it! You weep away!' he called, crying himself. 'Stop holding it all in. What's the point, eh? What's the effing point?'

Forty-one

June's positive mental attitude reinvigorated my night-wandering. The penny *had* been a sign. Ti wanted me to find her. And I wouldn't give up until I did. If Ti had something to do with the fire like people were saying (or Ophelia, more likely) then it made perfect sense for them to lie low.

Things in the hedges seemed to slither, but I had my staff for protection, and Ti's necklace clenched in my fist. The coast path lay ahead of me, thick and silvery in the darkness, and I focused on my breathing, on the ground beneath my feet. It was still freezing, more like December than May, and I was glad of the flask of tea in my bag. It had seemed like extra weight at first, but I couldn't end the tradition now. It would be like stopping hoping Mum would get well.

The ground was slippy from the day's rain, and the beach was littered with layers of bladderwrack, and as my feet started aching my P.M.A. began to fade. Ti could have left the penny under the Petrified Lady at any time. Years ago, even. Maybe some other kids had played around with it. I was fooling myself to see it as a sign.

Daphne's bench was nearby, and I aimed for that. How long had it been since we sat there together? Long before we went to Chase's garden and Ti started at The Bridge. It must have been about a year ago, when Ophelia was rehearsing for *West Side Story*, even, because we had seen her and Will earlier that night.

It had been a Saturday, I remembered, because Fab and June had gone to see a Queen tribute band at the Pink Coconut, and Ophelia had sneaked Will into the house. They had just become official, and he'd taken Fab's car round the block, to prove he could drive, and none of us could believe his nerve, except Ophelia.

'Told you he wasn't a square,' she said to Ti, and soon after he returned we had to leave them, because their public displays of affection were too loud and gruesome to tolerate. We'd taken snacks from the fridge, and walked to listen to the sea instead.

With Ophelia's profiteroles stickying our fingers we'd promised to meet here always, at Daphne's bench, even when we had white hair and Zimmer frames and those little grey old-people terriers.

But she wasn't out here now. I was delusional. I'd already checked Daphne's bench twice, why would a third time be any different? I was just punishing myself, because I'd lost the only real friend I'd had. Still, I couldn't go home without checking one last time.

The seahorse necklace was sweaty in my hand as I turned down the trail to Durgan. Except this time, Daphne's bench wasn't empty.

There was something on it, a shape in the dark, like a small person lying down, and I rushed to look closer.

My heart beat so loud the stars could hear, and I was so happy I could cry. It *was* a person! There were the legs, and the head: they were curled up, on the bench.

Weren't they?

As I drew nearer, what had seemed to be a head tucked into a body became only a lump. A sleeping bag.

The sea rushed in and out, down below on Durgan Beach, and its repetition was ominous and dangerous.

I lay down on the bench, and cried.

Forty-two

'Rosie?'

A figure crouched in front of me, icy fingers lightly touching my cheekbone. I had fallen asleep, and for a second I thought I was dreaming. She was so unfamiliar.

'Titania?'

She wore a big Puffa jacket I'd never seen before, with a rip on the shoulder where off-white stuffing spilled out, and I leapt from the bench.

'Ti!'

'Rosie!' she said, and it was so good to hear her voice. I wrapped my arms round her, and her jacket was cold and silky against my face, as she squeezed me back. We sat down together, drawing the sleeping bag round us, and the tears I'd been crying when I fell asleep were nothing compared to the floods that hit now.

'Oh my god, Ti. I thought I'd never see you again. I've been so scared!' I could hardly get the words out, and I thought I might throw up. 'What's going on? What happened? Are you okay?'

She closed her eyes, like there was too much to begin, and her teeth chattering made me remember the tea I'd packed.

Taking the full flask lid, Ti held it close to her face, breathing in the steam. As she drank I saw that her face was cut, with bruising over one cheek. Her mouth looked swollen too. Surely Fab didn't do that?

'We need to get you warmed up.'

'I've got to get back.'

'Back where? Where are you staying? Are you staying at Will's?'

She flicked her head to me abruptly. 'Why would you say that?'

'I went to see him when I first heard, and he acted weird . . .'

'Shit!'

'Listen, it doesn't matter. No one else noticed. It's just me because I've known him forever. Look, Ti, come to my house with me. I'll make you a special sandwich, and you can sleep in my bed. Joey will be so happy to see you.'

'*Rosie . . .*'

'I mean it, come with me. We'll sort this out. Joey never believed you were dead, not for one second.'

'Everyone else does, though, don't they? Everyone else thinks we are?'

'I didn't. Your parents don't. I went to see them, Ti, they're—'

'Please! Don't talk about them!'

'Okay, fine. But I'm just saying . . . I mean, I was scared, but I know how good a swimmer you are. It didn't make *sense*. And then I found the penny—'

'We need everyone to believe it.'

Your parents will never believe it, I wanted to say, *and the police are suspicious of your dad*, but she seemed so delicate in that moment that I daren't. I was terrified of losing her again.

'Please just come with me. You could leave before sun up, no one would even know—'

'I started the fire, Rosie.'

That shut me up. 'No.'

'Come on, you must know this. Mia saw me on school property just before.'

I shook my head. 'I don't believe it.'

'Well, the police will. My fingerprints will be all over everything. Drama block's destroyed. And what if Chase dies? How can we come back? How can we face anyone? The whole town will hate us.'

What did she mean *us*? She wasn't telling me the half of it.

'Chase is gonna get better,' I said. If I could just get her to agree to come somewhere warm with me, I could find out what had happened later.

234

'How do you know? She's seriously injured. Will tried to visit, but he wasn't allowed in.'

'Charlie told me he'd seen her! She said her room was full of flowers.'

'What, you're surprised that Charlie Fielding's lied? You're not allowed flowers in the ICU, insects can get in and put extra stress on the immune system. No, it's family only, apparently, which means it's bad. And what about the building? All the equipment? What if she's *scarred*? Or injured, properly injured. We can't *stay*, not now . . .'

There was that 'we' again. A coughing fit overtook her, and she covered her mouth with her hands. She was such a bad liar! There was a whooping sound in Ti's throat that sounded bad, and Daphne's bench was sucking the last of the warmth from my body. We needed to move.

'Just come home with me, Ti. We can sort this out. I'm sure we can. You can't stay out here with the weather like this. You've just got to tell the truth, that's all. Say exactly what happened, that it was an accident. It was an accident, right?'

She rubbed violently at her face, reminding me of her dad for a second. 'Don't be stupid, Rosie. No one will believe it was an accident.'

Ti had wrapped her arms round herself, and staring out to sea she looked like she didn't care if she was ever warm or comfortable again. 'I can't leave the coast path,' she said. 'I can't risk it.'

'I know you can't. I get it. We'll . . . We'll go to Kiaru's. His summer house has a heater. He's got one of the gates.'

'Nobody else can know, Rosie. Ophelia will kill me if she knows I'm talking to you.'

'Nobody will know. His garden's massive, and the summer house is right at the opposite end from the house. We'll just stay there for a bit, warm up, then you can go back to find her.'

'It's such a mess, Rose. You don't want to get involved. It's better off me and Ophelia.'

'Don't say that,' I said, holding her hands and trying to pull her up, and she didn't exactly jump to her feet, but she could have resisted more.

'You just have to tell me what happened. *Exactly*.'

Ti looked as though she was going to start, but no words came out. Her lips were turning blue. I shuffled closer, one arm round her back, and her Puffa jacket crackled against me. We put our heads down against the northerly wind that seemed to be building again, blowing the spiky gorse branches into us as we navigated the narrow path.

'When you're warm,' I said. 'Tell me when you're warm.'

Forty-three

Cups from my last visit littered the low wooden table, and I turned the heater high as it would go. The fan roared, and I had to remind myself how far we were from the house, and what human ears were capable of.

'You'll be warm soon,' I said, because Ti's teeth rattled loudly. She sat down on the gingham settee, and I put the patchwork blanket over her, then the sleeping bag on top.

'Ophelia will worry if I'm away too long.'

'She'll be wrapped up in Will. Take your shoes off.'

Ti scowled, because I was right. She leant forward to untie her laces, and there was a vinegary damp smell, and I saw that her socks were soaking wet.

'Dry them in front of the heater. I'll bring you clean stuff tomorrow.'

She draped the soaked rags on the edge of the table, and put her feet up, letting out a sigh of relief.

'I'll go back soon,' she promised herself. 'Soon as I've warmed through.'

I settled down on the floor in front of her, covering myself with the extra flap of sleeping bag. I took her hand, and closed my eyes. 'I'm so sorry for not being there for you, Ti. It'll never ever happen again.'

'I thought you hated me.'

'Of course I don't . . .'

'I know I'm not easy . . .'

'Don't say that, Ti, it wasn't your fault. It was mine, but I'm going to make it up to you. I'm going to sort this out.'

'You can't fix this, Rosie, no one can.' Her voice was soft, falling to sleep already, but I didn't know how much time I would have with her. Without Ophelia too.

'Ti, you have to tell me what happened.'

'I know, I will.'

'You have to tell me now.'

I couldn't see her face, but she took a deep breath.

'You have to give her a break, though, like you would me, because she didn't mean for it to get out of hand. It was so windy, d'you remember?' I remembered Kiaru's warm hand holding mine, and pink petals falling, his smell of deodorant and incense.

'There were so many things in the run-up, when you know the full story. It wasn't just one thing.'

'Go on.'

'So you have to listen.'

'I will, just tell me.'

'Okay . . . so you know there was a row, a big one, at home, and Dad, he . . .'

'Is that what the bruises are?' I asked very timidly because I was frightened of the answer.

'No! God, no – I'll get to that – this was earlier, teatime, just after I called you. Ophelia jumped out of our bedroom window, and I ran after her as soon as I realized. I knew she'd be heading for Will, so I walked to school, but by the time I found her she was a wreck. She'd been drinking Dad's whisky in her room, and she was shouting her mouth off, I couldn't get her to stop. She was shouting for Chase to come out and face her, and I thought she was going to get arrested she was so loud, but the play was loud too. We could hear it blasting from the gym, and nobody came out.

'I managed to calm her down, saying I'd go and get Will if she'd let me have the whisky, and she was just crying, sitting under the crab-apple trees, and she seemed to be snapping out of it. I left her listening to Charlie and Alex wrecking "You're the One that I Want", thinking I might be able to grab Will, but there were kids on all the doors, and I didn't want to leave her long, so I ran back, thinking I'd just make something up, but when I got there she'd gone.'

'Shit.'

'She'd had this parcel with her, things Will had given her – those stupid Twilight books, and her red scarf, and some letters – she'd been carrying it with her the whole time, and when I got back from my lap, she was crouched down by the Drama block, watching it burn.'

I turned to face Ti. She held her top lip as she talked.

'I knew it wasn't you! For god's sake, Ti! Why did you say it was you? And why do you have to leave as well?'

'I haven't told you the whole story yet. It's more complicated than that. The fire was partly my fault. Partly Will's fault too.'

'How? That doesn't make sense. From what you just told me—'

'You promised to listen.'

'Okay, fine, I'll listen. Just don't hold anything back. How did Will get involved?'

Ti's voice lowered. 'Because we saved his life . . .'

Forty-four

'It turns out they'd been planning to leave for weeks. Phe hadn't told me because she didn't want me getting into trouble if Dad found out, but the plan was to leave after the show, and then, out of the blue, Will just said it was too much, that he couldn't cope with the secrecy.

'Phe didn't believe him – they had everything ready, all their stuff packed in his shed – and she didn't understand what had changed. She thought it must be because of Chase, and Will admitted it.'

'What, they actually *were* having an affair?'

'That's what he said, and that's when she came home, in bits, and started attacking us all, and it just got out of control.'

'I can't believe it.'

'Yeah, but he was lying. He just said it to get rid of her, because she wouldn't believe anything else, and he was scared. Because it turns out that Dad had caught him after he left the bakery – earlier on – and grabbed him round the neck, and told him he'd better end it.'

'How did Fab find out?'

'Sophie told him. Somehow Charlie knew.'

My stomach turned over as I remembered telling Kiaru and Alisha. Had I played a part in this whole disaster as well?

'Phe was meant to be meeting Will at his mum's car after the play, then they would collect their stuff from his shed and leave, so as soon as we realized we couldn't stop the fire, we ran there. I didn't want to, the alarms were going off and people were rushing out of the hall, and I was scared we'd be seen, but Phe wouldn't leave without seeing him.'

'I must have missed you by seconds,' I said.

'He was fuming when he turned up, and he knew straight away what was what because we were both hiding behind the car, but he took us to the shed anyway, so Phe could get her stuff at least, and she was giving him loads of shit, threatening to report Chase to the police and calling him a coward and a cheat, and he was just silent all the way, in this old-fashioned suit with his hair slicked up.'

For the first time I wondered at what precise point in the play the alarms had gone off, and if the cast had managed to finish the performance they'd rehearsed so intently. Ophelia really knew how to cause a disturbance.

'I was in a daze, because I'd been rushing around for so long, panicking, and now the school was on fire, and I was on the run, and Dad had hit me. I was just watching the rain, which had started pouring, hoping it would put the fire out before it got too bad, and then, all of a sudden, Will started shouting back.

'We were on Castle Road, on that bend near the car park, and he just . . . lost control of the car. It veered left, and we went crashing off the road, through the trees down there. I thought we were dead. We were right by the spot where those girls went off the cliff last year – what were their names?'

'Emily and Amelia.' I said. I would never forget their names. Emily had been racing around the castle, like lots of the Beacon kids did, except she had misjudged the turn and was unable to stop in time, and her new car had gone careering off the cliff with her best friend in the passenger seat. The road had been designated a driving black spot, and speed bumps were scheduled. Amelia's grieving parents talked about it on Pirate FM quite often. They were the ones who had petitioned the council.

'Emily and Amelia, that's it . . . There were still flowers around the tree; I saw them as we passed. I saw everything. I could see branches ripping off as we hit, they were slowing us down, and then the car stopped,

just before we went over the edge – like something from a film – and me and Phe threw ourselves out, but Will was stuck. His seat belt wouldn't budge, and he was shouting, and the car just tilted there, right on the edge of the cliff, about to go over any second.'

'Jesus Christ.'

'It was insane. I still can't believe it. I was frozen. I couldn't move. If it wasn't for Phe . . . She was like an action hero; she knew exactly what to do. She pulled a piece of glass from the smashed windscreen and started hacking at the seat belt. Will was crying, like a little boy, telling her to hurry up, and all I could think was that the car was going to topple over with her still leaning in the window, but then she'd sawed through it, and we pulled him out, and less than a second later the car went.

'The noise it made, Rosie. It was so loud. It crashed on to the rocks – it was like an explosion – all the birds flew up from the reef. Will was proper white, like a ghost, he just lay completely still on the ground. We all did. None of us saying anything, getting soaked.

'It was his idea to leave our clothes on the beach. We all felt really calm, like we had to stick together . . . Afterwards, when the shock wore off. Will admitted he had been lying about Chase, and told us what had happened with Dad, and Ophelia admitted she'd started the fire. And it was weird. I can't explain it. We'd almost died, but we hadn't, and being alive was this huge

244

present, and we knew that if we had died, people would have forgiven us. For everything.'

Her necklace was still clutched in my hand, and I held it out now. She took it from me.

'You got a new chain,' she said.

'How did you break it? Did you rip it off your neck?'

'I can't explain. It was like we were becoming free of everything.'

'You wanted to be free of me?'

'I thought you wanted to be free of me! That's what it felt like.'

'I don't want to be free of you, Ti, I never want to be free of you. I'm so sorry I made you feel like that. I'm sorry for . . . what I said. About . . . prison.'

'Maybe you had a point,' Ti said, sitting up. Reaching behind her head, she fastened the necklace, settled it to rest between her clavicles. 'Anyway, thank you. I don't know . . . It seemed right when Will said it, like the only answer.'

'And how about now? Does it seem like the only answer now?'

Ti shrugged, too wrapped up in her story. 'Will sneaked back into his to get some of Charlie's old clothes, and me and Ophelia got undressed, and then we paddled along the shore to the rocks so our footprints wouldn't be in the sand, and it was so cold I thought we were going to die, and then Will brought us this stuff to put on.'

'And what about now?' I said, again, pushing. 'Do you regret it now?'

'No,' she said. 'I don't want to go to The Bridge and I don't want to work in the café. No one here likes me – except for you and Phe, and she's not going to be here any more anyway . . . and you've, you know, got other friends.'

'Not like you. None like you. Dad took my phone, you know. I didn't see your calls till after.'

Ti shrugged. 'It's okay.'

'It isn't,' I said. 'I should have been there. Maybe none of this would have happened.'

'Maybe it would have been worse,' she said, and I imagined Ophelia on the rampage without Ti following her about.

'So how come you're still here?'

'Will's getting a car for his birthday. We're going to drive to London, and find somewhere to live.'

'Really?' I wanted to say how unrealistic that sounded, but Ti could hardly keep her eyes open. 'When?'

'Saturday. There's no going back, not now,' Ti said, and her voice was soft and sleepy, her breathing shallow. 'Not unless . . .'

'Unless what?'

'Chase gets better.'

'I'm going to make it up to you,' I said, and Ti murmured something I couldn't catch.

Resting my head against the arm of the settee, I watched steam rise from her socks in front of the blow heater, while fog crept up the windows.

'I'll go and see Chase for you,' I said, but Ti's breathing had shifted. She was fast asleep.

Forty-five

The hospital was up the road from school, a big concrete fronted building that I'd visited lots of times before Grandad died two summers ago. Inside it was white-painted and busy, with medical staff charging to and fro. Non-medical people looked blank-eyed or sad or super-charged: a girl on crutches, a gowned man with magazines.

My heart galloped, another day at the races, but I was getting used to it. I breathed in my new way, in and out slowly. My only idea of how Chase was, and where she might be, had come from what Charlie had said, and she'd been lying. Grandad had been so thin at the end that you could feel his bones when you hugged him, and walking to intensive care without a breaking heart felt lucky and wrong in equal parts.

Waiting rooms, corridors, optimistic murals intended to distract dying people. Plants, a bald toddler, over-cheerful parents. I exited the lift with a doctor smiling over his text messages, and sneaked through the door that he was buzzed through without him noticing.

The carnations I'd bought on the way slipped in my sweating palm as I arrived at the nurse's station. 'I'm her niece,' I said to the severe-looking woman that questioned me. She had thick blonde hair scraped into a huge donut on top of her head and broad shoulders.

'Is she doing okay?' My voice sounded hollow, and for the first time in my life I wished I were better at faking, that I'd paid more attention in Drama.

'Oh, she's in good hands, hen,' she said with a thick Scottish accent, friendlier than she looked. 'What pretty flowers! We'll have to find another vase for the waiting room, they can't go into the ICU – well-loved lady your auntie, isn't she? It's chock-a-block in there with cards and flowers and balloons. But I can't let you see her.'

I froze.

'I'm sorry, poppet. Nice try, but I have it on good authority that Ms Chase is an only child. No nieces or nephews, though they do keep turning up. It's sweet, but your teacher's very ill. Last thing she needs is a load of teenage germs getting to her. We're very careful here, hen; we have to be. I'll find that vase, shall I?'

She took the flowers, as I was backing off, away from her knowing smile, and into the nearest toilet.

I *needed* to see Chase for myself. To collect the facts for Ti. I'd woken her before dawn, and she'd leapt up in a panic and rushed back to Will's shed, but before she left I'd promised her that this evening I'd have news she could trust.

After splashing cold water on to my face, I rested my forehead on the mirror. My hair needed washing, and I had bags under my eyes, and I remembered something I'd heard Ms Chase say dozens of times before: to be a good actor you have to fool yourself. I needed to channel my panic over Ti and lack of sleep into concern for my poorly aunt. Perhaps every staff member wouldn't be so well-informed. Perhaps I could fool somebody.

P. M. A. This nurse *would* let me pass. Forcing my feet to retrace their steps, I walked to try again. This time it was a different woman, older and more distracted, and I smiled sadly, remembering Grandad and how it felt in those last visits with him. How I still regretted not hugging him more.

A tear rolled down my cheek, and I didn't wipe it.

'I'm here to see my godmother, Laurie Chase,' I said.

'Good for you, and did they make sure you used the antiseptic wash on your way in?' she asked, and I nodded, turning my head away as I caught sight of the blonde donut bobbing around in a half-curtained area just to our left.

'She's quite poorly, so be prepared,' she said, coming out from behind the desk. 'It's good to keep a low-key reaction, if you can. Talk as you normally would.'

The nurse lifted her ID card to the sensor, and we were through into the ICU. Chase's bed loomed ahead of me, like the danger room at the end of a nightmare.

Patients were enclosed in separate capsules, and I could see them lying under pale blue sheets. No one did a crossword, or watched TV or listened to music, like Mum since her illness struck. These people were solely recovering. That was the only activity taking place here.

The nurse led me to the last capsule on the right. A body was propped up against pillows, and at first I thought it must be the wrong person because this couldn't be Ms Chase.

Her head was wrapped in bandages, and she was alone. Her face tilted to the left, mouth open and out breaths audible, a tube led from her nose, and her eyes were closed. A machine beeped out her heartbeat.

The shock of it made me jump back from the bed.

'She's on a lot of painkillers for the burns,' the nurse said. 'But you can still read to her or talk to her. That's what her mum does.'

I nodded, shell-shocked – *Ms Chase had a mum* – staying back, near the entrance to her area, I knew I shouldn't be here. 'Is she going to be all right?' I managed

251

to say, and the nurse squeezed my shoulder before looking me in the eye.

'She's not out of the woods yet, doll, but she's being very brave, and you need to be brave too.'

Beep . . . beep . . . beep . . . beep . . .

Sweat poured from my palms and I wiped them on my jeans. It hadn't been real when I bought the flowers. I had been focused on Ti. I hadn't understood. Intensive care wasn't for ill people; it was for people who might die.

The kind nurse's mouth was moving, worried about me, but I dodged out the way, as she reached forward to offer comfort. I didn't deserve to be consoled. I was a horrible little liar, and Ms Chase was a real person with a mum, like anyone else. Ti was right; I couldn't fix this. And I should never have come.

Forty-six

Dad came to wake me from a too-long pretend nap at one o'clock, and my stomach chugged with dread. I was due at June's and Fab's to discuss my speech. They'd rung as I arrived home from the hospital to ask if I would read at the vigil, calling me Ti's greatest friend and their honorary daughter with such affection that I'd burst into guilt-ridden tears and agreed at once, though I had no idea if I could manage it.

Setting down a cup of tea, Dad told me how proud he was that I was stepping up finally, and speaking my truth, and when I mentioned a stomach ache I thought his head was going to fly off his neck. His ears went red, and he told me to not *even think about it*, and ordered me out of bed right now.

After making me a fried-egg sandwich – 'Protein will give you energy' – he walked me all the way to the De Furias' though it was the opposite direction to the university.

'You're a good girl,' he said, knocking on the door. 'You've just got to resist this urge to do nothing all the time.'

June told him I was a little treasure, and I wished it were true.

'I bought sfogliatelle,' June said when Dad had left and I was struggling to take my shoes off in the hallway. My fingertips were sweaty and I couldn't breathe. When had I become such a fraud? Fab smoked by the back door in his grubby grey dressing gown. My heart beat fast, making me twitchy. I didn't deserve sfogliatelle. If the opportunity arose, I would sneak it out to Ti. But perhaps she didn't deserve it either.

Coffee boiled on the stove, and June rushed to remove it from the hob before Fab had a go at her for scalding it. Though perhaps those days were over.

The candlelit vigil was the next evening, and June talked about the arrangements so far. The weather was promising to hold – a gift from god, she said – and she'd been worrying about whether they should buy candles or if people would remember to bring their own, and then St Benedict's Church had stepped in and offered to provide tea lights for the evening.

'We're so happy to have you speak, Rosa. You're such a good girl,' she said, but I wasn't. Had I ever been a good person? Or had I always just been a sneak? Lying about who I was and keeping secrets that shouldn't be kept.

The girls are safe, I wanted to say. *I saw Ti last night. This whole thing is a sham.*

But June was on to her next question, about how many candles would be needed, and it was a tough one, because the De Furias weren't the biggest collectors of friends, especially the young ones.

'How many do you think will come from Fairfields? A guestimate,' June asked shyly, and my heart sank.

'Quite a few,' I offered, and June's sad eyes sparked a little, inspiring me. 'Yes, quite a lot, I'd think.'

Fab threw his cigarette over the fence, and spat in the drain.

'You don't have to lie to us, Rosie; we've had enough of that. We love the truth round here. New policy.'

I looked at my feet, and June tutted as she poured milk into a pan on the hob.

'They were little pigs sometimes, June, and you know it. Especially Ophelia. Takes after her effing father.'

'*Fab!* I mean it. Stop now. All morning he's been like this: negative, every word that comes out his big mouth. Ignore him, Rosie, please. *Ignore him.* Maybe the girls weren't nice to *every single* child at school *every single* day of the year, but people like to give second chances. People like to think they'd get a second chance themselves. Wouldn't you agree, Fabio?'

Fab sat at the kitchen table, and closed his eyes.

'My friends Alisha and Ava and Kiaru will come,' I

said, wanting to give something that was true, however puny. June looked pleased as she poured the coffee.

Kiaru didn't call any more, but this morning he'd sent an email telling me they'd be at the vigil, along with an attachment of an orang-utan cuddling a koala. We'd talked about it once, odd pairings of different animals, and whether there was anything better. I sent back a tiger and a bear, wondering if he'd still want to email me if he knew I was hiding my best friend in his garden. If he knew the real me. (Who even was that?)

At June's insistence Fab showed me the leaflets they'd had made: the same birthday picture of the twins, with the words HAVE YOU SEEN US? at the top, and then details of the vigil printed at the bottom. My eyes were drawn like magnets to the question, and I thought I might gag.

'Take some with you,' June said, and I took them in silence.

'Alex Riviere printed those for us,' June said. 'He got in touch with Pirate FM too. He's going on the radio tomorrow, to put a call out. He's friendly with one of the DJs apparently. Poor boy, he's quite distraught. I think he might have a soft spot for our Ophelia.'

Fab harrumphed, and June shot a look at him that said quite clearly: *don't you dare.*

She pulled a plate of sfogliatelle from the oven, and with a determined expression turned to me. 'Eat them while they're warm,' she said, and her hand visibly trembled as she added milk to our gold-rimmed cups.

Fab took the darkest pastry, and shoved half of it in his mouth. With flakes on his lips he spoke, and his voice was soft and quiet, like I'd rarely heard it. 'Nothing tastes the same without the girls, does it, eh? Pigs or not.'

June dipped her head, leaning over to wipe at Fab's lips with the cuff of her cardigan, and my mouthful of cream and pastry turned to cat litter on my tongue.

Forty-seven

'I can't keep your secret,' I said to Ti.

It was around one o'clock in the morning, and we had just arrived at the summer house, were sitting on the sofa with the heat turned high. Ti refused to look at the flier Fab had given me, twisting her body away when I put it in front of her face. 'Please don't, Rosie. I feel terrible as it is.'

'No, you need to know what you're doing.'

'Stop it!' She grabbed the flier from my hand and scrunched it up.

'See! You couldn't do it, if you knew. If you could see your mum and dad, you wouldn't be hiding like this. They haven't given up on you, you know. And they're never going to.'

Ti closed her eyes.

'I went to see Chase too.'

'Oh my god.'

'I wanted to have something good to tell you, that's why I went, but there isn't anything good, and I shouldn't have gone. She's not out of the woods yet, that's what the nurse said. She's got breathing apparatus, and bandages all over her face . . .'

Ti had her head in her hands.

'People are accusing your dad of . . .'

'Don't! Will already told us; we know all about it.'

'And it's okay with you is it?'

'No, but . . . you know. It's not like they're going to find our bodies, is it?'

'Can you hear yourself? What you're saying? Your dad's not shaving or getting changed out of his dressing gown, Ti. They're thinking of selling the café. I mean, are you even sorry?'

'Of course I'm sorry!'

'Because I think, if you could just *see* Chase and your mum and dad, you wouldn't be able to do this, what you're doing now, what you're planning. What *Ophelia's* planning.'

'Everything's so black and white with you, isn't it? Ophelia bad, Titania good. Phe's right, you don't get it.'

'No, Ti, it's you that doesn't get it. You're not helping your sister by doing this. Do you think everything will just be all right when you're in London?'

'Rosie, stop it.'

259

'No, I'm serious. What makes you think there won't be any more "accidents"?'

'*Rosie*. You're wrong about me. You think I'm better than I am. You always have.'

'No. *You're* wrong about you, Ti! *I* know exactly how good you are.'

'Rosie . . . I need to tell you something. In the garden that time, with Chase—'

'No.' I sat back on the sofa, pulse racing. I knew what she was going to say.

Ti swallowed, visibly nervous. 'You've always thought so well of me,' she said. 'I couldn't bear you knowing . . . that I—'

'No!'

'I wish so badly that I hadn't.'

'So Chase isn't a liar? You did threaten her?'

Ti nodded.

'What's wrong with you? Why would you even do that? What did you say?'

'I said that she didn't know who she was dealing with. That she didn't know the kinds of people I knew. I was just trying to stop her from calling the police!'

I felt my mouth open in disbelief. Not for one second had I believed Ti was capable of threatening a teacher, and yet somehow her confession wasn't entirely shocking.

'You should have told me.'

'I know. I was ashamed. I could hardly admit it to myself.'

'You should have trusted me.'

We sat for a while in silence. It was another clear night, and out of the window of the summer house I could see the waves of the ocean reflecting the moonlight.

'Poor Chase,' I said after a while.

'See. I'm not who you think I am,' she said. 'I'm not a good person. I'm broken.'

'You're not broken, Ti. You made a mistake, that's all. You were stupid. But you didn't start the fire. You don't have to take the blame for that. You don't have to disappear.'

'Part of the reason Phe was so convinced about the affair was because she thought Chase had lied. I tried to tell her, that night at school, but she wouldn't believe me. She thought I was just saying it to calm her down.'

'Ti, listen to me, you're not to blame for this. Ophelia is the one that set the Drama block on fire. There's no excuse for doing that – can you not see?'

'But what would we look like? Coming out of hiding after what we've put our parents through? It's got too big, Rosie. We've caused too much trouble.'

'People like to give second chances; they like to think they'll get them for themselves. It's true. Isn't it?'

Ti cocked her head to the side, and I felt hopeful for a second.

'I can't do it, Rosie. I can't do it to Phe.'

'And what about what she's doing to you?'

We could just about hear the sea from here, rearranging the stones at Durgan again and again like the world's biggest obsessive compulsive, and I forced myself to say the thing I'd been thinking for a long time, that I'd never dared say before.

'Ti, what if your sister needs proper help?'

'She just needs to start again,' Ti said too quickly. 'We both do. A fresh start, that's all. Listen, I'll talk to her. I'll see what she says. Just promise me you won't do anything. Not until then.'

Forty-eight

Durgan Beach was fuller than on a hot day in August. Near the cliffs to the east, on the rocks where the girls had left their clothes stood Dad's sound system and generator and a tower of speakers. From Will's shed Ti and Ophelia would be able to hear the speeches. That's what I'd latched on to as the sun rose. Too agitated to sleep I'd written my speech, trying hard to work out what I wanted to say. What I *needed* to say. What combination of words must Ti hear to realize what was right?

Here and there candles in jars flickered against the dark, and the sea rushed in and out. Dad held a clipboard and answered questions, and I couldn't help smiling. He and his activist friends wore T-shirts emblazoned with SISTERS COME BACK, and I was glad he hadn't listened to me when I told him being on their side now made him look like a hypocrite.

A banner with the same words hung from a table full of bottles of pop and plastic cups that Mum attended to, seated in the deckchair Dad had set up for her. Her medication seemed to be working, and she had persuaded Dad to let her try attending tonight. 'How could I miss our daughter's first speech?' she'd said, and Dad had caved.

It was like fireworks exploding inside my chest, seeing how much effort people had made. There was no way Ti could leave when she saw the turnout.

Joey was babbling about what he was going to say when she revealed herself. He was going to give her a cuddle, and then tell her off, but not too much, because she would already be feeling bad, plus her mum and dad would be planning to tell her off properly . . .

Walking here, the streets had been busy with a mixture of kids from school and people from Ti's church, as well as a handful of overweight customers I recognized from bleary mornings waiting for Ti at the De Furia café. There were teachers and shopkeepers too, though no sign of Kes or Ms Chase. Her absence hovered over proceedings, and I wondered how she was. Dad swore that when it came to hospitals no news was good news, and I hoped that he was right.

Kids dodged around in gangs, setting up little games and making the most of being allowed out late. They ran and whooped, wound up by the idea of a disappearance, while curious detached adults sipped from paper cups. Dad had made it into an event.

A canny student had cycled down a freezer and generator and was selling ice creams to a growing queue of excitable kids, and Joey tugged at my arm, begging for money to get one. I found a pound in the bottom of my bag, and off he went, fist tight round his money, positive things were going to turn out okay. It was only two minutes to Will's shed from here, I could see what Ti was making of all this, while Joey queued.

It was tough running up the narrow cliff path with all the oncoming traffic, but I made it, scanning the hedgerows as I went. The wild area around Daphne's bench was clear too. There was just the odd cluster of people now; most of those who were going to attend had already taken their places. The attic light was on at Kiaru's house, which made my stomach flip, but the summer house was empty. Too early for Ti to be there.

Will's house looked empty too, as I let myself through the gate. There was nobody in the shed. Or so I thought, until I looked down to find Will, Ti and Ophelia huddled together on the floor beneath a blanket.

'Effing hell!' Ophelia gasped. 'We thought you were Charlie.'

'She's been following me,' Will said, standing, and brushing dust from his front. 'She knows something's up.' From their lack of shock I knew Ti had told them we'd been meeting.

Will picked a bag from a pile, and made for the door.

Ophelia's eyes were bright, and her cheeks flushed even in the low light. Ti wasn't looking at me.

'What's going on?' I said.

'Road in two minutes,' Will said. 'Not a second more.'

Ophelia grabbed him in a hug, and laughed, and Will reached over to Ti and clamped her head in his palm, the way I did to Joey sometimes, and she dodged out his way, a reluctant smile on her face.

'Ti, what's going on?' I said again, though it was obvious. Will nudged past me, preparing to dash through his garden. 'What about the vigil?'

'What about it?' Ophelia said, at the same time as Will said: 'It's the perfect cover.'

'Won't it look suspicious if you're not there, though, Will?' I pleaded.

'Two minutes,' he repeated.

Joey was going to be heartbroken. I couldn't even think about Fab and June.

'Ti, you can't do this. People are coming out for you.'

Ophelia sneered. 'They're coming out for themselves. They're only sorry because they think we're dead. Soon as we're alive we're criminals.'

'You're a criminal anyway! Jesus, Ophelia. You set

fire to the school! And how long do you think you'll be able to hide for? Ti? Are you never going to see your mum or dad or me or Joey again?'

'Oh, just go away, would you? This is nothing to do with you,' Ophelia said, picking up a huge rucksack and pushing past me. Ti stood with her arms limp at her sides, eyes cast down.

'If you go now, I'm going to tell everyone you've been hiding. I'll send them chasing after you.'

'You haven't got the guts,' Ophelia said, walking away perfectly confident across the garden.

'I bloody have!' I called after her.

She scoffed, and I felt a hand on the small of my back – 'I'm sorry' – then Ti hurried past me too.

'Ti, *please*,' I said, following her.

'I can't do it,' she said, hurrying forward. 'I *am* sorry. I just don't want Ophelia to go to prison. I don't want to be hated even more. "No more strikes", that's what they said last time they picked her up. And I got a warning for being *at Chase's house*. What if they make it look like it was premeditated?'

'Ti, you didn't start the fire.'

'The only way I can stay is if I say I did, though,' she said. 'I've thought about it all day. Do you want me to do that?'

'That's not the only way you can stay! Stop saying that!'

From the beach floated up the sound of June singing

'Ave Maria', and Ti dissolved into tears, backing away from me.

'That's your *mum* down there,' I said, because we both knew how much it must have taken for June to get on stage. Her voice was so full of hope. How could Ti do this to her? In the road a horn honked, and I could imagine Ophelia reaching over Will to press it.

'If you cared about your sister at all, you would make her face up to this.'

'I can't. I'm sorry,' she said. 'I can't do it. Please don't tell everyone, Rosie. *Please*. They'll hate us.'

And then she ran after her sister, the same way she always had, and I wanted to scream because she was so pathetic, and how had I ever followed her anywhere? Sprinting back to the coast path to find my brother, I didn't care if anyone saw. What was there left to lose? Crushing my speech into a ball as I left Will's garden, I lobbed it into the hedge.

Forty-nine

Joey grinned, offering me what was left of his ice cream. 'Not long now,' he said, falling into step beside me. He looked confused when I refused the flake he'd saved.

You won't see her again, I wanted to say. *Ti is leaving right now, and I don't know how to stop her.*

But that wasn't true. I knew exactly how to stop her, I could whisper in June's ear or tell Dad or grab the microphone. *She's been hiding. I've been hiding her. Will is driving them out of town; we can catch them if we leave now.*

But what Ophelia had said rang in my ears. As soon as people knew the truth – especially if it came from me – they would see them as criminals. The girls were forgivable if they were dead or missing. But not if they came back. Where was the logic in that?

Joey put a sticky hand on my arm, wanting to know what was wrong, but I was trapped with my thoughts. I should have told the truth that first day, instead of making promises I couldn't keep because I felt guilty. Now I'd backed myself into the same corner they had. Why wasn't I able to think ahead? Why did I always get it wrong?

I hated Ti. No wonder I'd been so easily distracted by Kiaru and Alisha. Ti was a disaster. She acted so different when Ophelia was there, like I wasn't important at all. And did she really believe she was helping her sister? It was exhausting watching her make a mess of every chance anyone gave her. I was sick of it. Sick of her.

Joey licked his ice cream beside me, and I felt like such a gruesome phoney down here at the vigil when the twins were on their way out of town. They would cause trouble in London, and nobody would be there to pick up the pieces. No parents or money or friends. The gorse threw out the smell of coconut, and the sea turned the stones on the shore, and I knew I'd never enjoy a day at this beach again.

My lip hurt and I realized I was biting it. I *knew* she didn't want to go, but she wouldn't say it and it made me so mad. All this time I'd thought she was strong, because she looked out for me, but she was weak. She was even weaker than I was! How had I never realized?

I scanned the candle-carrying people filling the beach, my eyes searching nervously for June and Fab. How could I face them? My involvement no longer seemed kind or noble. It was impossible to remember what I'd been thinking.

We were right by the makeshift stage that Dad and his colleagues had built from crates and scaffolding planks, and I closed my eyes, wanting to kick at the tiny stones and shout at the sky, because I was such an unbelievable idiot. I'd gone along with someone else's plan when I should have spoken up. *Again.* I was still doing it. The same coward I'd always been, that I'd always be, getting it wrong over and over.

Julie from Dad's department walked through the crowd, handing out candles to those without. She squeezed my shoulder as she passed me a tea light in a jar, and it was a shock to feel something outside of me, I was so deep in my own thoughts.

Joey let go of my hand, and bolted over to where Dad was standing, giving out fliers, and then I saw them.

Fab and June.

Hopeful smiles plastered on to their faces, arms stiff and hands clasped together. My stomach flipped, and I made a dash for Dad.

'Rosie!' Fab was heading through the throngs of people towards me, candle in hand, June a step behind, her expression suddenly animated.

He pulled me into a hug – the first one he'd given me since before Chase's garden – and I thought I would die, but June was next, and I could feel her fast bird-like heartbeat as she clasped me to her.

'You've done such a good job!' she said, and her voice was so cheerful I could have cried. 'Your dad knows so many people!'

'We couldn't have done this without you,' Fab agreed, his deep voice cracking as he pulled me in for another hug. 'I'm sorry, I wanted to be strong, not cry, but it's hard. All these people . . . and then you, Rosie, cuddling you, you feel just the same size, the same shape as, as . . .'

June pressed her lips together in apology, and began whispering to Fab who nodded, eyes scrunched shut, and I pointed in the general direction of my dad, backing away and heading over to him, stumbling over the layers of rocks. I couldn't go along with this, and I couldn't confess either.

Joey leapt out from where he had been crouching, and I thought I might puke I jumped so much.

'Got you!' he screamed. 'Got you! I got you! I got you!'

'Have some respect, Joseph! This isn't a party,' Dad hissed at him, and Joey toned down his grin, but his eyes still sparkled.

He looked at me for reassurance, but I was all out.

'Rosie?' He pulled against me, dropping all his weight off the end of my hand.

'What if they have gone, Joe? What if they really have gone?'

272

'Not possible,' Joey said, but his eyes had changed: glitter shifted to wood. His mouth was pressed firmly into a line, and he held his own weight again.

'No!' he said, stamping his foot, as if scolding a dog.

People jostled all around us, pushing forward as more made their way on to the beach, and then the microphone screeched and Dad was up on the stage.

'Thank you for coming! Thank you so much for coming here tonight in solidarity for our missing girls: Titania and Ophelia De Furia. And thank you to June, for that emotive performance. We are all extremely hopeful that the twins will return, and I would like everyone to bear this in mind as they light their candles tonight – lighters are making their way around, don't worry – this is not, I repeat, *not*, a memorial.'

Fab and June stood to the left of him, at the side of the stage, clasped together like a pair of teenagers. Tears ran down Fab's face and June's lips moved fervently, the fingers of her hand not held by her husband clutching rosary beads, and my heart hurt with all their wanting. I wondered if Fab was really going to speak, and if I would be able to stand it if he did.

The road out of town would be quiet now. Everybody who was coming would be here or close by, everyone else tucked away in their houses. Will was right: it was the perfect cover. Soon they would reach the bypass.

If I spoke up, we could catch them. But it would

confirm all of the worst charges against them as well. Ti might never forgive me. But if I didn't speak, they would be lost. And Ophelia would be right about me.

Dad talked on, but the babble in my head was so violent I couldn't understand. Somebody lit my candle, and I stared at the flame. All around me people clapped, and Dad stood with the microphone held out, eyes resting on me as he waited for the next speaker. The crowd looked at me, and it was like a nightmare – *what did they want?* – and then I realized.

I'd asked to speak early because I was so nervous. I'd thought I would be speaking up for Ti, finally, saying the things I should have said a long time ago. Deep down, I'd thought that somehow she would be here, in the crowd or listening on the coast path, I'd never believed she'd be able to run like that.

The audience applause was running dry, expectant. It was like falling into a dream, and the flamethrowers threw, but what did that matter? It was dark, and clouds rushed overhead in a smooth grey stream, and I had no idea what I was going to say.

Letting go of Joey's hand, I walked onstage.

Fifty

Hundreds of faces peered at me, candles twinkling, and I wondered how many of them had been kind or helpful to Ti before tonight. How many would be willing to give her a second chance? Silence across the beach, except for the disrespectful gulls, and looking around I saw Kiaru and Alisha huddled together near the caves. Charlie and Mia sat on a rock to the back of the beach, looking skeptical, and Charlie's eyes were wet, but I couldn't tell if she'd been laughing or crying or was drunk.

My eyes flicked over the familiar faces of the crowd, and I lifted my chin. I wasn't scared of any of them. My voice, when it emerged, was flat, but I couldn't alter it.

'I threw my speech away, because it was lies. I was going to thank everyone for coming, for making the effort, and all that, but I don't feel grateful, to be honest. I feel angry because it's too late. None of you cared about Ti or Ophelia when they were here. Maybe you were right not to . . .'

I froze, looking at my feet.

The words wouldn't come.

'This whole thing's a sham. I'm sorry, I can't do this.'

I blew my candle out, unable to go on with the charade, unwilling to look at Fab and June or Mum or Dad or Joey, not wanting to see their response. Ophelia was right, I didn't have the guts.

Dad stepped on to the stage, and put his arm round me and I felt my brother's small hand slide into mine. Dad and Joey blew their candles out in solidarity, and we stood together, dazed, looking out at the yellow flickering faces on the beach as one by one flames were extinguished, until there were hardly any left, and we stood in silence in the dark, seagulls shrieking.

Joey wrapped his arms round me, and I leaned on the top of his sweet-smelling head. Dad had taken the microphone, and was trying to cover up the awkwardness, talking about emotions running high, and how we shouldn't lose hope.

A noise had begun somewhere near the back, people were leaving, thinking the show was over, and I hated them for not caring enough. Not caring when it counted. But I understood too because more than anything I just wanted to go home. To put on my pyjamas and climb

276

into bed and pretend all of this didn't matter. That I was blameless.

People whispered amongst themselves as they left the beach and I kept my head down, never wanting to let go of Joey, and then a voice, far away.

'Wait!'

The crowd gasped, peering into the dark at a figure running down the coast path.

People moved out of the way, murmurs rising to exclamations, and then they started to say her name.

Joey had his head back, and his arms raised as though he had just finished an incredible routine in a gymnastics floor show.

'YES!' he shouted, his voice filling the beach. 'YES!'

Tears streamed down her face, footsteps echoing around the cliff top, it was Titania, wiping at her nose with the back of her hand as she ran.

June barged through the crowd, tugging Fab along in her wake.

Joey tried to make a dash for it, but Dad and me held him back at the same time.

'Not yet, Joe,' Dad said.

Grabbing her parents' hands, Ti kept running, the three of them heading for me, and my whole body was electric with relief and joy, as my best friend and her parents stepped on to the stage. Ti took the microphone, which still dangled in Dad's hand.

'Hey,' she said breathlessly.

A few people said hi back, uncertain. She put her hands on her knees for a second to get her puff back; she never had been much of a runner.

'Thanks for coming.' She gulped. 'Sorry for . . . all the trouble.' She let the microphone hang for a minute, wiping at her face. 'The rumours are true. I did start the fire. But it was an accident.'

Knowing looks and whispers sped around the audience, and I took her hand and squeezed it. She'd come back; that was what was important.

'You can think what you like about me,' she said, her voice getting louder, as she turned to look at Fab. 'But my dad is a good man. And he deserves a second chance.'

Her voice cracked, and tears ran down Fab's face, as he pulled Ti into a bear hug. A few people in the audience clapped, and I saw Mum wiping her eyes, seated at the front, in her deckchair. Joey grinned beside me.

'I'm so sorry,' I could hear Fab saying. 'I'm so sorry. My littlest girl.'

Ti pulled away, still holding Fab's hand, and the microphone screeched, causing Dad to shoo her away from the speakers.

'I wish I could say I was brave enough to stand up here like this because I love my dad so much, but the truth is I almost left, I was in the car. And if it wasn't for my best friend, Rosie Bloom, I wouldn't be up here. She told me that people like to give second chances because they want them for themselves. And I wanted to find out if that was true.'

Her parent's gazes shot to me, and then June reached for Ti's necklace. She lifted it for a second and I didn't know where to look as the silence expanded.

And then, gradually, the audience began to clap. I saw Mum, on her feet, and Kiaru with his hands in the air. Dad's flame sputtered back to life, and then Joey's. Lighters making their way from person to person, until there were dozens flickering against the night, and over by the caves Kiaru and Alisha grinned at me. Kiaru put his fingers in his mouth, and a piercing whistle rose above the applause.

People laughed and cheered, and held each other, and I cuddled Ti, who sobbed against my neck, until her parents took over. I jumped off the stage to stand with my family, who crowded round me, kissing my hair and cheeks and ears. People's faces were soft in the candle-light, and the sea fussed around us, like a concerned aunty, and onstage, with their heads bent together, in a hug that seemed never ending, Ti, Fab and June.

Fifty-one

Dad, Joey and me were packing away the beakers and banners and rubbish when the hug finally ended, and Ti made her way over. Her face was difficult to read, a mixture of relief and sadness, and I was glad, because the way I felt was complicated too.

Dad pulled Joey along with him to collect any rogue paper cups littering the beach, and I could hear my brother complaining, furious to be removed from the action, but I was grateful to have Ti to myself. I didn't want to have to fake our reunion. I was done with all that.

We walked to the caves, where Kiaru and Alisha had been, to the rock we liked to sit on in summer if Durgan wasn't too crowded. The beach was mostly empty now, except for our families who stood together, talking and clasping hands, and we watched them for a while.

'Thank you for not telling,' Ti said, and I bit my lip.

'Ophelia was right. I didn't have the guts.'

'You've got the guts,' Ti said, looking me in the eye.

I shook my head. Something was rising in me, something that I'd held down a long time.

'I haven't, Ti.'

'You have, you just chose not to use them.'

'I never confessed to Kes.' I blurted the words out, and my heart was in my throat. 'I tried, but he brought up Mum, and I didn't want to make things worse at home. I'm so sorry, I felt horrible about it but I couldn't do it. Ti?'

She had picked a handful of stones, and was sieving them through her fingers, like she didn't know what to say, and I felt more worthless than I ever had, because she'd stood up there and made out I was some kind of hero.

'Look, Rosie, I already knew you never owned up. It was obvious after the appeal.'

'Oh. Really? Why didn't you say anything?'

'I knew my lie about Chase was worse. I thought maybe you . . . Suspected.'

I leaned back onto my hands, and looked at the night sky.

'Let's just never lie to each other again, okay?'

'Okay,' Ti said, and I realized in a deep and sudden way that she was more Daphne than I would ever be. She was more Daphne because she loved the sea for what it really was underneath.

'I'm glad you came back,' I said, but Ti's smile was weak, and I knew she was thinking of Ophelia. 'You did the right thing.'

'I hope so.'

'You really going to take the blame?'

'I'm partly responsible.'

Picking at a patch of seaweed, I wondered if I was partly responsible too. It could easily have been my fault that Fab discovered Will and Ophelia's relationship. Nobody knew until I confided in Alisha and Kiaru. But there was a difference between telling a secret, and making a threat and starting a fire. Still, I was finished arguing. Ophelia was Ti's sister, and that was that.

I took Ti's hand and squeezed it, and she squeezed it back, and then June, Joey and Dad were walking towards us, with Fab struggling to push Mum in the wheelchair Dad had borrowed from the university, over the pebbly beach.

Yodelling, Joey tore away from Dad. He held Ti as though he would never let go.

'Why'd you set fire to the school, though?' he said, as he pulled away. 'I'm going to have to pay out, like, seven pounds forty. You owe me.'

Dad swiped at the back of his head and Joey ducked.

'Took balls,' Dad said, to Ti. 'Getting up there in

front of all those people. We were wrong about you, Titania.'

'You're a good girl,' Mum said. 'And Alistair's right – you must have a labia of steel, confessing onstage like that!'

I couldn't keep a straight face, but Ti looked sombre, like she was receiving a medal from the Queen.

Fab and June beamed proudly, and Joey side-skipped around, as though herding us all to stay together.

Fifty-two

Later that night, Ophelia returned too. Mum, Dad, Joey and me were eating Fab's lasagne at the café when she walked in, shivering, mascara smeared beneath her eyes. Her parents and Ti hugged her, laughing and crying, but she only looked blank, and I stayed out of her way.

Ophelia hadn't been able to let Ti take all the blame, but she wasn't happy to be back, and I felt sorry for her.

The Friday before summer term started Dad got a call from Kes. Chase was out of intensive care, and well enough to discuss my fate, and they had decided to give me another chance at Fairfields, seeing as I had the potential to be a good student. They had learned of my innocence regarding the distribution of the posters, thanks to Alex Riviere, who had confessed in a moment of conscience.

At school I was famous by proxy. Ti and Ophelia

had taken on legendary status, as though risen from the dead, and everyone thought it was me who had made them come back. It was well known that I'd taken the photo of Chase and Kes too, even if I hadn't put up the posters, and somehow it was a good thing. People asked me about nightwandering, and laughed at my jokes, and paid attention as I walked around the school. Turned out Alisha was like Joey when it came to secrets.

It was Ophelia who had convinced Alex to put the posters up, and I felt sorry for Charlie Fielding. Alex had dumped her after he found out that she'd encouraged Ophelia to think Will was cheating with Chase. He went out of his way to be nice to everyone these days, and avoided cliques. Most of the time, he devoted himself to rugby training.

Fab and June adored him because of his help when the girls were lost, and he often tucked into complimentary pizza at the café when I was waiting for Ti. Ophelia sneaked him cakes and pastries, too, watching him eat with the determined expression I knew so well.

I still hadn't spoken to Kiaru properly, and I felt so weird about it, but I didn't know what to do. I hung around with him and Alisha every day, but Alisha talked so much that we didn't get chance. She had ended things with Ava because they got too serious too fast, and she wanted me to set her up with Ti, who she swore was as gay as a dancing flame. Kiaru seemed happy to let her dominate, and I guessed it had ended, whatever we had begun, until one day I found a drawing of a tiger and a collie in my school bag.

The next day, I put a postcard of an ostrich and a giraffe cuddled together into the back of his Maths book in a flurry of Ti-encouraged daring, and when he came to find me after the lesson finished I understood the phrase *jump for joy*.

Fifty-three

I still hadn't spoken to Ophelia when her court case
came round months later. She had admitted arson at an
earlier hearing, and today the decision would be made
as to whether she had intended to set the fire or not. Her
solicitor had prepared us for the worst, and Ti was sick
with fear. She was a witness, and was terrified she would
send her sister to prison.

Mum was well enough to come downstairs most days
by now. She set about finding things to distract me, like
animal clips or new music she'd discovered or flapjack.

By lunchtime I was so restless that she persuaded Dad
to drive me to the city so I could be there when Ti came
out. How must she be feeling if I was this twitchy? Mum
made sure I looked as neat as possible, even though I
wouldn't be allowed in court, combing my hair so that it
turned into a fuzzy eighties-style frizz that she thought
looked smart. She brushed the fluff from my least

worn-out cardigan, and I tried not to be embarrassed by Dad's faded cords and scuffed moccasins as we walked into the pillared courthouse.

'Don't feel bad about me not having court clothes,' he told me when I wished aloud he had a proper jacket. 'It's a good thing.'

We sat in the waiting room, joint-reading a newspaper, and drinking chicken Cup-a-Soup from a vending machine Dad had found, until eventually June and Fab emerged from the court. There was no sign of Ophelia, and I guessed that the worst had happened. What would I say to Ti?

Then I saw the two of them, clinging on to each other, just behind their mum and dad. Ophelia looked particularly beautiful with her long dark hair tied back in a low ponytail, and without eyeliner or lipstick she'd lost her untouchable edge. She was unable to hold in her sobs, and June nodded her head happily, as she saw us.

Ophelia had been sentenced with a Youth Rehabilitation Order, which meant no prison but a lot of other conditions, and looking around at her family she seemed as gentle and law-abiding as June.

Everyone hugged Ophelia's solicitor, apart from Dad and me, and then Ophelia hugged her again, and all of them were talking at the same time, while we stood awkwardly by, Dad kneading my hand.

Fab was in bright yellow trousers, which made me feel a little better about my Dad's gormless outfit, and Ti was wearing her black and white café uniform with the dorky black patent work shoes she hated so much. Only Ophelia wore a new dress, charcoal grey, with a white lace collar that brought out her Italian side.

She was still too overwhelmed to talk when we went into the street, but June told us that Ms Chase had been a revelation.

'We didn't even know she was going to speak! She'd asked to be there, and she was allowed, as she was involved in the case, but we had no idea. I'm sure it was her that made the magistrates lenient, you know. Absolutely sure of it.'

Fab had one arm round each of his daughters, and seemed to have lost the power of speech, while June was more talkative than ever. Youth courts didn't allow members of the public, as a general rule, or I would have insisted on attending myself. Luckily, June couldn't say enough about it. She'd even taken notes.

'She said it had been a privilege to teach Ophelia, and that a more "passionate, rambunctious young woman, you would have trouble finding". What else did she say, Phe?'

Ophelia shook her head. She was staring at the stone steps we were standing on, as though she couldn't trust them to hold her, sticking very close to Ti.

'It was her that did it, I'm telling you . . .'

June turned the page of her notebook.

289

'Right. "She wasn't the most academic kid, but put her on stage, and she would give you goosebumps." That's what she said. And that if it was up to her, all charges would be dropped, and medical advice sought. Sorry, Phe, I shouldn't have read that bit. She thought it was "an act of passion entirely without serious consideration by an emotionally unbalanced teenage girl, and it would be disastrous for her future if she were to be made an example of."'

It was clear from the power of Ophelia's relief that she hadn't expected this outcome. None of us had. Ti hadn't slept properly for weeks.

Holding her mum's hand, Ophelia looked like a harmless little girl, and it was hard to compute exactly how much damage and disaster she'd managed to create.

Fifty-four

At the bottom of the stone steps we stood in a circle, winding down the conversation before we went to our separate cars. I'd said goodbye to everyone except Ophelia, who seemed to be purposefully avoiding my eye, and I was trying to work out what the best thing to say might be, and how to go about it, when she appeared in front of me.

'Hey,' she said stiffly, and her eyes were pink and swollen as she wiped them.

'Hi.'

Ti and our dads had made their way down the stairs to the roadside and were swapping ideas about possible routes home, though there were only two that anyone knew of. Ti joined them as they talked about the weather, which was doing that thing of being everything at once, and the price of bread, which had gone up again, apparently, and I was grateful to her for giving us space.

'I owe you an apology,' Ophelia said, surprising me, and I thought how amazing real apologies were, because all of my resentment towards her drifted away from wherever I had been holding it, and all I wanted was to give her a hug.

Up close, her hair smelt the same as Ti's: like pina colada.

'I know you think I'm such a bully and Ti doesn't get a look in, but it isn't like that. I love her. I'd do anything for her.'

'I know.'

Ti was trying her best not to watch us, but I could see her ears twitching. She had her head slightly angled in our direction, and a fake half-smile plastered on her face as she nodded at something my dad was saying.

'I was angry with her at first, for making me come back. Because she *knew* I wouldn't let her take the blame – you didn't, and Will didn't, but *she* did.

'That's what people never get about us: they always think I'm the boss because I blow my top, but Ti gets her way too. She just goes about it differently. That's why it took her so long to decide, because she was deciding for both of us. Because, *as if* for one second, I was going to go let her take the blame.'

I looked at my feet, unused to hearing Ophelia talk like this. I wanted to say something so we could stay in this new world of openness, but everything seemed inadequate.

'So . . . are you glad you came back?' It wasn't earth-shattering but it was real at least. Something I honestly wanted to know.

'Oh, I was always going to come back. I was just angry with everyone. I wanted them to think we were dead, and feel sorry, and I was under Will's spell. I've wanted to run away with him for so long! God knows why, he's the most self-obsessed person in the universe . . . I think he only went out with me in the first place to piss off his mum and dad.'

'Well, I'm glad you came back.'

'Really?'

'Yeah. And I'm glad you gave me such a hard time about Ti too, because I deserved it, and I didn't even know.'

'Huh. Well. Maybe you were a good friend to her. I mean, in the end.'

Ophelia's eyes flashed as she looked at me, and I felt that mine were bright too.

Fifty-five

We were walking to our separate cars when a sharp voice I hadn't heard in a long time called Ophelia's name. Across the road a small, striking woman with a shimmering turquoise headscarf stood beside the river.

Ms Chase lifted her hand, bright scarf flapping where the tails hung loose at the back of her neck.

Ophelia ducked her head, as she walked over to meet her, and cars slowed to let her pass, which was lucky because she crossed the road without even glancing at the traffic.

'I'm so sorry,' we heard her saying. 'I'm so, so sorry,' and I was shocked at the emotion in her voice.

Ti was near enough that I could feel the warmth of her arm through my cardigan, and I remembered how happy Ophelia had been when she was cast as the lead in *West Side Story*, and how brilliantly she'd played the part. Her nervousness at being on stage had come across as a tough kind of shyness, and for a while she had been Ms Chase's indisputable favourite. They used to walk around together at break: Ms Chase, Ophelia and Will, talking about the best ways for them to bring their truth to the characters of Maria and Tony.

'What do you think she's saying?' Ti asked.

We were all silent, as we watched the two of them sit on the bench on the grassy verge opposite the courthouse: Ophelia turned towards her ex-teacher, while Ms Chase stared straight ahead.

Ophelia was clearly thanking Ms Chase for speaking up for her, clasping her hands together, but what was Ms Chase saying? None of us could imagine. Ophelia nodded continually, and then Ms Chase reached round the back of her head, and I felt like I was creaking up the highest part of a roller coaster, about to cross the threshold before hurtling downhill at ninety miles an hour.

With a flick of her wrist Ms Chase had tugged the turquoise scarf away.

Her hair was short all over like a tough boy's, and she turned in her seat to face Ophelia, holding herself very straight, sharp chin jutting out. She ran her palm over her bare head and Ophelia stared, then leaned forward. And as Ms Chase rested her hand between Ophelia's shoulder blades, rubbing her old pupil's back, I wondered what it was about her that we could so have hated.

Fifty-six

'No, let's go to Daphne's bench,' I said to Ti. It was two in the morning on the first Saturday night after Ophelia's sentencing, and we were making a special sandwich. The plan was to nightwander, but we couldn't decide where. Getting up when the alarm went off had been difficult, but I'd forced myself.

'I'm tired,' Ti had grumbled, and I'd almost laid my head down again, but something had made me insist, and now we were in the kitchen, dressed in black, assembling a sandwich. Ham, cheese, tuna, mayonnaise, mustard, peppers, sweetcorn. It was a good one, and seeing it stand there, sliced diagonally to showcase its multicoloured layers, we were tempted to eat it indoors.

'No. Let's go to Daphne's bench,' I said, pulling tin foil from the drawer, and laying a sheet on the breakfast bar. I lifted the sandwich on to it, and Ti watched as I wrapped.

'A present for us to share very soon,' I said.

The crinkling of foil was loud but Mum, Dad and Joey were asleep upstairs. The town slept all around us, except for next door's new puppy, Chip the paranoid insomniac, and it was odd to be purposefully, effortfully awake, like we used to. As I handed Ti the parcel to put in her rucksack, and waited for the tea to brew, I could tell she felt it too.

The sky was clear above the empty terrace, and without agreeing our strides grew longer. We headed for the coast path. Below, the boats made knocking sounds as they rocked in the harbour. The ever-present seagulls swept through the blackish blue, and as we left the sprawl of the town, all reluctance vanished, and the freedom feeling grew.

The coast path wasn't wide enough for two, and I increased my pace. I wanted to show how unafraid I was. How unnecessary torches were with night vision as powerful as ours. Laughter rose from the beach, students round a fire, and I thought how sad that sound would have made me when I was marching this stretch alone.

'I've got an interview for St Anne's on Monday,' Ti said, as we began to climb. Below us, the beach turned to reef, then cliff, and I thought of Sophie's car tumbling over; of Will, pale-faced, lying in the woods; and Ti and Ophelia, breathless and heroic, getting rained on. Of poor unlucky Emily and Amelia.

'That's brilliant!' I said, but it sounded false. Ti attending a different school while I was at Fairfields still made me squirm.

'I'm going to work so hard,' Ti said. 'And then I'm going to go to the marine college.'

I tried again. 'That's really, really brilliant, Ti.'

The muscles in my thighs ached, but I pushed on. It felt good to be outside and awake while everybody else wasted their time unconscious. Like we knew a secret. The turn-off to Daphne's bench was ahead, and the old feeling of anxiety fluttered in me, though Ti walked metres behind.

She told me how Ophelia refused to talk about what Ms Chase had said to her, as though it were too precious to share, except that it was partly Charlie who had convinced her to make a statement.

'She must have felt really guilty,' Ti said.

We walked in silence for a while, and I wondered if Chase had always been good, and we had just misjudged her, or if she'd become a better person because of everything she had been through.

Arriving at Daphne's bench we unpacked our sand-wich, and the night broke and soared and glittered around us. There was something I needed to know, and it was difficult, but I had to ask.

'Ti . . . was your statement true? About Ophelia?'

Ti didn't look at me, and her expression was grave, curly hair blowing across her face.

'I don't know. I mean . . . how do you set fire to a building by mistake?'

We stared into the dark, and something thrilled through me, starting in my stomach and spreading up my ribcage and then running down my back, because she trusted me again, now I knew. I took a bite of my sandwich and leaned against her, paying attention to the peace all around me, and the warmth of her, right there.

'Did you leave the penny for me to find?' I said. To use its full title, *the Penny of Old*, seemed suddenly embarrassing.

Ti smiled at me, and her cheeks were even bigger than usual as she chewed.

'I couldn't believe it when you found it. I felt like a crazy person, turning it over. I was sure Ms Chase was going to die, and either me or Ophelia were going to have to go to prison, and I needed not to be caught if our plan was going to work, but I saw the Petrified Lady when I was walking and I couldn't resist. I felt like George in *Five Go Adventuring Again*, except I was also the villain, a big babyish villain.'

'Did you ever tell Ophelia?'

'Course not,' Ti said, laughing. 'She'd have killed me. I just said you had had a hunch.'

We weren't identical twins, we weren't even blood sisters, but what we were was better, because we had chosen it. We were best friends, and we had secrets of our own, and if I needed her to she would lie for me, like she might have lied for her sister, like I would have lied for her.

The sea at Durgan far below reflected the moonlight prettily and underneath the little white peaks of thousands of waves, bladderwrack floated and jellyfish drifted and seahorses did their daily dance, a whole world under there, that I, up here, could only imagine.

LOVED

night

WANDERERS?

READ ON FOR A PEEK AT
C. J. FLOOD'S AWARD-WINNING

Infinite Sky

'Extraordinarily powerful . . .
brilliantly visual and full of feeling'
GUARDIAN

Infinite
Sky

C. J. FLOOD

WINNER OF THE BRANFORD
BOASE AWARD

Prologue

You can't tell that the coffin holds the body of a boy.

He wasn't even sixteen, but his coffin's the same size as a man's would be.

It's not just that he was young, but because it was so sudden. No one should die the way he did: that's what the faces here say.

I think about him, in there, with all that space, and I want to stop them. I want to open the box and climb in with him. To wrap him up in a duvet. I can't bear the thought of him being cold.

And all the time the same question flails around my head, like a hawkmoth round a light-bulb: Is it possible to keep loving somebody when they kill someone you love?

One

It was three months after Mum left that the gypsies moved in. They set up camp in the paddock one Sunday night while we were asleep. My brother Sam was excited when he saw them.

'Gypos!' he shouted.

Sam used to have a gypsy in his class: Grace Fitzpatrick. She'd been famous at school because she could do as many things with her feet as with her hands. She could even write her name with them, which was funny because she couldn't read. Sam, who'd sat next to her in assembly, said she smelt like cat piss and fire smoke.

'They live off barbecues,' he told me as we watched from Dad's bedroom window.

I thought it sounded brilliant.

There was a caravan and a clapped-out car and, a few metres away, a fire with a pot hanging over it.

'Be bloody hundreds of 'em by the end of the day,' Dad said, emptying sawdust from his overall pockets onto the floor.

'They'll probably tarmac the field while we're asleep,' Sam said. 'Try and make you pay for it.'

Dad made a growling noise. 'Be a nightmare getting rid of them, that's for bloody sure.'

He left us leaning on the windowsill.

Sam made dents in the wood with his fingers while I wondered what Dad was going to do. This was exactly the sort of thing Mum would have sorted. She'd have been best friends with the gypsies by breakfast, had them falling over themselves to make her happy, even if that left them without a home.

'Look at all those dogs,' Sam said. 'Bet they fight them. Tie blades to their paws.'

I shook my head.

'Seen it on the telly,' he said.

'What, on kids' telly?'

He dug his elbow into me until I squirmed.

Two greyhounds bounded round the paddock and I tried to imagine them snarling at each other, blades flying, but it was ridiculous, and then the caravan door swung open, and a tiny black dog scurried out.

A woman appeared in the doorway. Tall and thin, with red hair falling over one shoulder, she looked beautiful. She lifted her arms above her head and stretched, revealing a stripe of tanned belly beneath her green vest. Behind her the white caravan seemed to sparkle.

'Prozzie,' Sam said.

The woman spun round suddenly, and a teenage boy in rolled-up jeans leaped from the caravan, laughing. He'd obviously startled her. The three dogs ran over to him, the tiny black one lagging behind, and he bent down to tussle with them. They licked at his bare chest.

Sam didn't have anything to say for a second. The boy looked about the same age as him. He was clearly the woman's son, tall and thin like her, but with lighter, ginger-blond hair that flicked out above his ears and curled on the back of his neck.

'Bet *he* don't go to school,' Sam said.

'Come on, Iris,' Dad called up the stairs. 'You're going to be late.'

'Aw, shame,' Sam said, because he was on study leave.

Still, I couldn't help staying a minute longer, watching as the red-haired woman filled a bucket with water from the pot above the fire and began scrubbing her steps.

Dad left the house at the same time as I did. With fists clenched, he headed towards the paddock.

* * *

I couldn't wait till the summer holidays. Everyone at school was getting on my nerves. *Especially* Matty. At registration, when I told her about the gypsies, she told me this story about her second cousin's boyfriend's brother: he was on his way to the newsagent's to buy a magazine when a gypsy girl burst out and cracked him over the head with a golf ball in a sock. For no reason. I told her we didn't have any girls, only a boy, and described the way his hair flicked out, but she curled her nostrils at me.

'Pikeys are gross, Iris,' she said. 'You'd get gonorrhoea.'

Matty was always name-checking STDs. She thought it made her look sophisticated.

At dinner time, we watched the boys play football.

'Your socks are odd,' Matty told me. 'Don't you care?'

'Not really.'

'Maybe you should.'

I took my shoes off and folded my socks down so their oddness was less obvious.

'That's your problem, Iris,' she sighed. 'You think that makes a difference.'

Before maths, next lesson, I nipped into the toilets and took them off.

Matty had moved to Derby from Guildford four years ago with frizzy black hair and too-big glasses which left red dents on her nose, but every new term she got prettier. Today her black frizz was tamed into long waves that she twisted round her little finger. Her glasses had shrivelled to contacts, and to make matters worse, her boobs had gone from a size nothing to a 32B in the last six months. As far as Matty was concerned, she was a fully mature woman.

'Remember, Iris,' she'd taken to saying to me, '*my* birthday's in September. *Really*, I'm in the year above you. *Really*, I'm a Year Ten.'

Every day, after school, I watched the gypsies. They hadn't listened when Dad told them they weren't welcome, and much to his annoyance were getting on with their lives. As well as the teenage boy, the dogs and the red-haired woman, there was a man, a baby and four little girls.

The boy spent a lot of time with his mum. He got in her way while she was cleaning, and made her laugh. Sometimes she grabbed him and ruffled his hair. They reminded me of how Mum and Sam used to be.

The gypsy boy was good to *his* sisters. They were all loads younger than him, but he still played hide and seek with them, and picked them up when they cried. I couldn't imagine him getting mad at them for something as silly as borrowing his socks.

In the evenings, they all sat around the fire, or on the grass nearby, until it was time to eat whatever their mum cooked in the pot, or their dad brought home in the car. Later on, when the mum had put the little ones to bed, the gypsy boy went to lie underneath the caravan by himself, and I felt as though I understood him completely.

Dad shouted if he caught me watching from his bedroom window.

'It's not a game, Iris,' he said, and so I kept my spying to when he was out.

One night, I left my curtains open so the sun could wake me. I wanted to see what the gypsies did first thing. It was well before six when I crept upstairs, past Dad sleeping with his head half under the pillow, to my usual perch on his armchair by the window. He didn't notice. Mum was the light sleeper – the snorer too. She used to make herself jump in the night.

Underneath the early white sky, the paddock was dotted with poppies, and fat wood pigeons in the tall poplars surrounding the yard called to each other. The boy got up first. He jumped down the caravan steps and did a lap of the field with the dogs. Occasionally, he stooped to pick up sticks, or tugged dead branches from the hedgerows.

By the entrance to the paddock was a huge pile of logs that Dad and Austin, his apprentice, had cut down over the months – a year's supply at least. Reaching it, the boy stopped. He glanced towards our house, and I ducked behind Mum's rose pincushion cactus. I peered round its spiky dome, which was flowering purple, and watched as he added a couple of long, slim branches to his pile.

Back at the camp, he knelt to build a fire. By the time the door to the caravan next opened, he was fanning the flames with a sheet of cardboard. His mum emerged carrying a stack of bowls, the baby wrapped to her back, and the boy changed position to direct the smoke away from them.

'Eye?' Dad lifted his head. 'That you?'

Dad called me Eye, as in ball. Sam had started it. Mum used to tell Dad off for joining in, back when they still talked to each other. 'She's named after the flower,' she'd say, but she didn't mind really. It was just some-thing they did.

'What you doing?' Dad said now.

'Need some socks,' I said, pretending to rummage in the unsorted pile I'd been sitting on.

The plastic of Dad's alarm clock creaked as he looked at it. 'S'not even seven,' he groaned. 'Go back to bed.'

I watched the boy put on a rucksack, pat the baby's head, and walk to the far end of the field where the paddock dropped into the brook. He reappeared on the other side of the water, and then disappeared into the cornfields, and I wondered where he could be going.

* * *

I was sad to be leaving science for the summer. Biology was the best, not only because I got a break from Matty. I was in the top set, and she was in the bottom, and I paid extra special attention when Mrs Beever talked about the parenting traits of various birds. Apparently both male and female swans help build the nest, and if the mother dies (or drives off in a van to Tunisia) there's no need to spaz out and call the RSPB. The male swan is completely capable of raising his cygnets alone. I *almost* wished Matty was sitting next to me when I heard that.

All afternoon we bickered, but choosing sweets in the shop after school she still invited me to sleep over at hers that night. 'We can do a fashion show with my new clothes,' she said. 'Mum's making spag bol.'

'Doubt my dad'll let me,' I lied, putting ten fizzy cola bottles in a paper bag.

'He still being unusual?' she said, and I nodded, but the truth was I couldn't bear it round hers any more.

Her mum, Donna, asked questions with her best talk-to-me expression: Are you *okay*? And is your dad *okay*? And is everything *OKAY* at Silverweed Farm? The worst thing was that Matty didn't stop her. She just stood there expectantly, as if the two of them had become some kind of talk show mother/daughter duo, and I their favourite guest.

Acknowledgements

There are so many people I would like to acknowledge for their help and support along the way to finishing Nightwanderers. First and foremost my empathic and insightful editor, Rachel Mann, not only for her belief in this story, but for her suggestions on how to improve it, many of which can be seen throughout these pages. Also Jane Griffiths and Elisa Offord, as well as the whole team at Simon and Schuster for continuing to make my dreams reality. And thanks to Elv Moody for her encouragement in the early days of this book.

Thanks to Drue Heinz, founder of the Hawthornden International Writers' Retreat, for allowing me to stay at her beautiful castle in Scotland while I did the final edits for this book, and to Grants for the Arts for their generous support.

As ever, huge thanks go to my family whose belief in me never falters: Mum, Dad, Nanny, Liam and

Thomas. And to the friends who cheer me on, and who I couldn't do without, Fiddy Matthews, Skem Diddly, Nathan Filer, Emily Parker, Ursula Freeman, Molly Naylor, Em Prove, Alex Ivey, Sophie Sherwood and Elizabeth Mizon. Special thanks to Max Naylor who is my biggest inspiration and most beloved of the beloveds.

Final thanks to Catherine Clarke for the unwavering faith in my writing: it means a lot.